A TIDING OF MAGPIES

Pete W Sutton

For Claire. Always
&
In loving memory of W.E. Sutton

ACKNOWLEDGEMENTS

I'D LIKE TO express my deep gratitude to a few people who helped me on my path to becoming a writer. For Jo Hall & Roz Clarke who wrangled some early words into shape and in the process taught me a vast amount on how to put a short story together. For all the North Bristol Writers past and present for the years of support they've given me. For all the members of "The Pact" who workshopped several of these stories and last, but definitely not least, all the staff and contributors at Far Horizons magazine, who have kept me sane. Especially Kimberly Nugent who is an awesome editor!

Thanks also to Graeme Parker for seeing a potential in these stories and in me.

Much thanks to Sammy Smith & Grimbold Books for doing this second edition reprint when KGHH went out of business

CONTENTS

FOREWORD
BY PAUL CORNELL

I STILL SALUTE magpies. I can't help it. I'm not even sure why I do it, though my Mum always said it was 'for luck'. When I'm out with someone else, I need to turn the gesture into a little brush of the hair. I don't like to admit that I'm doing something out of sheer ingrained West Country habit, rather than for rational reasons or because of a supernatural belief system. The rhyme that starts 'one for sorrow' is meant to be the outcome of seeing that number of magpies, and thus I feel more inclined to salute just one of them, though I also tend to use that gesture to rule out joy, girls, boys, silver, gold, and on the rare occasions you get so many of those rather solitary birds together, secrets never to be told.

Pete Sutton, with this collection, has taken on that magpie rhyme from many different angles. A number of the stories are about children, a number of them could be called magical realism. They fit into that gap between rationality and magic. He's got a way with characterful dialogue, with ironies, with endings. Honestly, what more can you ask for from a writer? They pay us for endings. He reminds me a bit of Neil Gaiman, in that he enjoys the business of story itself, and shares that enjoyment with the reader rather than hiding secret references. His prose is direct, his approach engaging. You'll learn in these pages, for example, how Long John Silver lost his leg, and how a small boy was dragged into fiction to giddily witness that.

Pete has, in recent years, made his home in Bristol, and curated writing groups, events and launches for his fellows in that most hospitable and artistic of British cities. He's part of the furniture there, but it shouldn't be forgotten that he himself also has a talent for the fantastic, which is well-represented by the stories within these pages. Unto you I heartily commend them.

Paul Cornell May 2016

One for sorrow,
Two for luck; (or mirth)
Three for a wedding,
Four for death; (or birth)
Five for silver,
Six for gold;
Seven for a secret,
Never to be told;
Eight for heaven,
Nine for hell
And ten for the Devil's own self

ROADKILL

"One."

There's a pause of a few minutes.

"Two."

I'm annoyed and curious.

"Wotcha doin?" I say

"Countin."

"I can see that, wotcha countin?"

"Three."

He gives me a sharp look. "Them."

I follow where my little brother is pointing out the back window and see a red splash and what might be black feathers in a lump, disappearing behind us on the side of the road, lurid in the backlights.

"Ewww Gross! Mum he's counting dead things."

"Be nice to your brother, Mikey." Rote words, said with no inflection, she's not really thinking, she's concentrating on the road.

I almost say "But Mum!" when I see her glance in the rear view mirror. Her eyes make me stop.

It's not my fault the holiday was crap. Why did we go to the Isle of Wight anyway? Without Dad. Taking Granny. I cross my arms. What a crap idea. What a crap holiday.

"Four."

"You've got to be kidding, there's no way there've been four dead things," I start, but he gives me *The Look*. It's not right to be frightened of your little brother, is it? Although, if anyone ever said that to me, I'd punch their lights out. It's a good job he likes me.

"Five."

I look behind the car, I can't tell what it is but it's bloated and strange with legs sticking in the air like antennas. He looks at me smugly.

Granny is snoring in the front. She and Mum are the only ones, apart from me, that seem to be able to talk to him. Without him freaking out. That's why I call him, *The Horror*.

"Six."

"Seriously?" He gives me a look with his eyes almost rolling up into his head and makes a face. I know better than to argue.

"Why don't you boys try and get some sleep?" Mum says. So I close my eyes. All the better to ignore the little horror.

"Seven. That's a secret never to be told isn't it, Mum?"

"Uh huh."

"Isn't it, Mikey?"

I turn my back and make sleepy noises.

"Never to be told," he murmurs, quite close to my ear, I do my best to ignore him. The sound of the wheels on the tarmac lull me. I am comfortable. I drift off. The last thing I hear is "Eight."

Later I wake, sweaty and confused. It is quiet.

"Why've we stopped?"

There is a lorry on the other side of the road with its full beams and hazards on, in front of it, lying down and apparently nonchalantly chewing the cud, is a cow.

"Why's there a cow on the road?"

"Shhh go back to sleep."

"Need to go pee!"

"Mikey, take your brother to go to the toilet."

I sigh and get out of the car. I walk all the way round the trailer, which holds all our camping stuff, and open the door.

He is waiting. I take his hand and we walk over to the hedge.

"Not here, Granny can see." I turn to look and sure enough Granny is looking out of the window, seemingly at us, although you never can tell what's going on in Granny's head, or if she's looking now or into the past, or even the future. She's not been the same since Dad… well since it happened.

"Guh! Come on then." I take him deeper into the bushes.

"Turn around." We've played this game before. I know my part. I turn and gaze at the road and notice a set of headlights approaching fast. I see the lorry driver, or maybe it's the farmer, standing in the middle of the road. He's trying to flag down the car. It's going too fast. It swerves to miss him and ploughs straight into our trailer. There is an almighty bang and I see the trailer disintegrating and our car go up on its front wheels then back down with another bang.

I leave *the Horror* and run to the car. It's a mess - if we'd been in the back we'd be dead. Granny has lost her teeth and is bent down in the footwell looking for them; Mum looks white as a sheet. I stare at the car that hit ours. It's big, a Rover or a Mercedes or something. The guy staggers out. The car is skewed across the road partially blocking the light from the truck.

"Who the fuck decides to park on a fucking tiny country fucking road," he babbles, slurring his words, like Dad used to when he got home late.

"Is everyone alright?" I decide he is the farmer. He looks like one. Mum is just getting out of the car, she looks at me "You're all right." It's a statement, not a question. I look round for *the Horror*. He is stood just behind me, staring at the mess. Our stuff is all over the road.

"Nine." I look at him without understanding then slowly turn to look at the road. The man's car has smashed into ours then bounced off and hit the cow. He looks up at me "Nine is for hell," he says. He looks over at the man, "and ten. Ten is for the Devil's own self." He takes my hand as the man slumps down on the road pulling at his collar. Mum and the farmer are by the man's side. He's gone a funny colour, I can tell that even from where I'm standing, he's making small choking sounds that I can hear between my Mum saying "Are you OK? ... What's happening? ... it's just like Paul... can't you do something?"

Paul is my dad. Was. I mean, was my dad.

I look at my little brother and he is staring at the man, who is now lying down. My mum is shouting at the farmer "Do something! For God's sake, do something!" and crying. She used to cry a lot. When Dad came home all shouty and sweary and had to teach her a lesson.

The man is not moving. My mum is crying. I am standing at the side of the road holding my brother's hand. He looks up at me and says, "never to be told".

One for sorrow,

Two for luck; (or mirth)

Three for a wedding,

Four for death; (or birth)

Five for silver,

Six for gold;

Seven for a secret,

Never to be told;

Eight for heaven,

Nine for hell

And ten for the Devil's own self

THE STONE OF SORROW

'THE STONE OF sorrow is sharp, like a shark's tooth, and heavy, like a dead child. And the longer you carry it the more it cleaves to you.' Ma told me that when the old dog died; she wasn't wrong. I was about six or seven at the time and inconsolable. Of course it were worse when Ma died herself. Delivering us Emily, my last sister. Pa got drunk when she passed and hasn't been a day sober since. Left it to me and Mark to run the farm, Luke too when he's old enough. Ruth to run the house and Emily to help her when she's grown too. John's too simple to help with anything and Ruth's burden is to look after both him an Pa too. I'm Matthew, the eldest.

The farm is failing. We've put our best days into it, and our worst. But still it fails. Not a thing we can do about it. The weather nowadays has become all screwy and unless you have the cash to pay the mega agri corps for genned seeds you have to watch the old crops falter and fail. We talked about investing in livestock, but that's all it was. Talk. No cash to invest. Pa's debts are long and deep. Maybe if we ever get done paying for the harvester we'd have something.

Farm's been in our family since the civil war. Granted as thanks from Cromwell to our great, great, great several times grandaddy for conspicuous valour against the Royalists. Successful land too, rich and fertile. We done well out of it until now. In Pa's time the land began to fail. He made a few wrong choices and now here we are. Almost broke and new war coming.

When the army man came I was out in the fields sorrowing over the wilted crops, the rancid soil. We weren't the only farming family going through this. The soil everywhere was failing. When the recruiter asked, Mark said he was the eldest, so they took him. Should have been me, but then what would have become of the farm? I bless him and curse him in the same breath. The stone of sorrow cleaves ever closer.

I watched the storm clouds. Every so often glancing up at them, smelling the wind, racing against time. Trying to secure the soil before the acid rain came. Trying for barley next time. Ruth helped. All hands. Luke told to look after Pa. And John, and Emily. Big burden for a small boy. Still he's sensible that one. Older than his eleven years. He's learned about the stone of sorrow too. We all have. Well, apart from John and Emily. One too simple, the other too young.

Being a man down would be an even bigger burden if the crops hadn't failed. You can't farm dust so my days are mostly spent in despair and hiding from the others just how bad it is. I've got in the habit of making sure I wake before the rest of them so I'm first to the post. I've been hiding the letters from the bank. I know it's wrong to do so; that I'm burying my head in the sand. But it's a compulsion. I know it can't last.

This morning there were three letters. A red one from the bank, one from the company and one from the army. The one from the bank was a foreclosure. Unless I could pay them in the next fourteen days they would take the farm and we'd be homeless. The one from the army started 'we regret to inform you.' Mark had been killed, something to do with a training accident. There was to be no body to be buried though. A new transportation technology. Top secret.

The last letter was an answer; hope. The company were looking for volunteers for an experimental soil and seed treatment. Of course I couldn't afford to be cautious. I phoned the company straight away. They said they'd sort out the bank, send their men over forthwith. I'd saved the farm. Well that's what I thought when I got off the phone. It were a little more complicated.

The company rep arrived, bald, in a black suit - looked more like a man used to putting dead things in the ground rather than help take live things out of it. He explained that the company had bought out our debt from the bank. They owned the harvester now, and would sell it on. We wouldn't need it no longer. They owned the farm - if the experiment proved to be a failure. If it were a success we'd be allowed to live here to pay off the debt, by working our farm. Pa had to sign it. The company man wanted to witness, didn't seem too bothered that Pa was dead drunk and I 'helped' him sign the papers.

What if the experiment were a failure? Yeah, that. Then the land would be dead and no amount of coaxing would bring it to life. And we'd be out. They'd use the land to dump things, or build a power plant or something else but it wouldn't be a farm any more. Last throw of the dice; I was gambling everything on the experiment being a success. Even then Emily would be grown and married and have babbies of her own before I'd paid off that debt. But we'd stay in our home. We'd have an allowance. The company promised not to interfere in our affairs. But they'd install a foreman and a work crew here too. Although the work crew'd be robots.

You've seen them robots that go out into forests and cut down trees by themselves? Well these robots the company were bringing would till and plough, seed and harvest. The 'foreman' was a roboteer - a technician to keep the robots working. He'd take his orders from the company - but teach me how the robots worked so that when (if) the experiment were a success I'd run the crew next year, and for many years to come until we'd paid off our debt. The company reserved the right to change out any member of the crew for any reason at any time. Our farm, their lab.

I was expecting big machines, like our harvester. The company came and removed that one day. They didn't bother coming to talk to me about it. One day I came back from the fields and it was gone. A truck brought three robots the size of old time cars. They each had a large stencilled number on them and we nicknamed them Uno, Dos, Tres. The truck also brought Ramirez, the roboteer. She wasn't what I was expecting either.

She was around my age, maybe a year or two older - probably fresh out of college. Course I'd not been able to attend college so I hoped that learning about the robots didn't need any book smarts. She wore overalls, not too different to mine, cept hers were clean, and new. When she jumped down from the truck I didn't know who she was.

"You Matthew?" she asked.

I nodded.

"Here's some papers for your father to sign." She held out a thick handful of papers.

I raised an eyebrow. "He's already signed lots."

She gave a smile, friendly, I counted the freckles on her nose. "These papers are for these robots. Once he's signed them you can help me unload them and then Bob the driver can get going."

"You're the roboteer?"

She sighed and the smile faded, wilting cos it hadn't sparked one on my face. "Yes. I'm the roboteer. Can we get on with things?"

I held my hand out.

"I need to witness," she said.

It were my time to sigh. "Come on then."

Inside I introduced her to the family. Ruth were cooking, Emily on one hip. Luke were reading to Pa. There was no sign of John. "Pa? This here lady is from the company, she needs your signature." Pa grunted, long into his cups. If we got him first thing he wouldn't be able to sign cos of the shakes, now he was barely conscious. I helped him sign, just like before. Caught the twist of lip and wrinkled nose Ramirez tried to hide when I glanced her way.

"Luke, where's your brother?" I asked. John needed a lot of looking after.

Luke looked around. "He was just there, on the sofa, dammit."

"You go find him, now. I'll be outside with Miss Ramirez."

Ramirez gave me a raised eyebrow, her deep brown eyes asking a question.

"Let's go," I said.

She followed me to the yard where John stood gazing at the machines. "Hey buddy," I said edging close. "You should be inside."

John grinned in that way of his. You'd like to think there was some brain at work, but he'd never learned to talk, or any bowel control. Eight years old and still in nappies. "Hold on, Miss, I'll just take him inside." I could tell he was fascinated by the big machines. He played with the little toy cars I'd had as a kid, then Mark, then Luke. Although the paint was all rubbed off, and many missed wheels, he still loved them.

When I got back outside Bill, or Bob or whatever the driver's name was, hopped down from the cab and ambled to the back of the flatbed to drop the tailgate and ramp. Ramirez pulled a controller - looked a little like an old time game console, but with a big touchscreen as well as some buttons and a joystick. She tapped away on it for a few seconds. Glanced at me. "Once I've done the tricky bit I'll show you how to steer them." She looked over my shoulder. I turned. John stood at the open front door, watching the first robot come off the truck. "Luke? Goddammit, see to your brother." Luke appeared looking sheepish and steered John back inside, closing the door after himself.

After she'd manoeuvred the robots off the truck and the driver had gone - with even more signatures, this time from the company woman - Ramirez spent some time showing me how the controller worked. Once I'd watched her put Uno and Dos in the big barn she let me use it to put Tres in there too. When we got back to the house I noticed there were suitcases. I'd known that Ramirez was staying. I'd cleared out Mark's room. "Well," she said, "I'm calling it a night. Up at dawn to get to it." She held her hand out. Frowning I shook it. We stood looking at each other for a beat. "Well?" she said.

"What?"

"Where am I staying - give me the tour."

Once I'd shown her the bathroom, and pointed out the other bedrooms, John & Luke shared, as did Ruth and Emily, I had to put Pa to bed. He'd lost so much weight I could carry him like a child. He squirmed though, and his elbows were sharp. Like a shark's tooth I thought, as I got him to the bathroom. He'd need cleaning up before I put him in his bed. The door opened and Ramirez took a step back, startled, on the other side. She'd let her long black hair down. She took in the fact I carried my father and scooted out of the way. I glanced at her retreating form, she looked back over her shoulder before disappearing into Mark's room. Time to get Pa in the shower.

When I got to my room I found that I was too wired to sleep. I crept downstairs, the steps each creaking their own notes, and into the kitchen and grabbed a beer from the fridge. I took it outside and sat on the porch swing. Watching the night sky, counting falling stars, when a flash of blue light from the large barn caught my attention. Putting the beer down I watched the barn closely but there was no second flash. The first hadn't been in my imagination though so taking a last swig of the beer I levered myself off the bench and marched over to the barn to take a look.

I took the torch down off the wall next to the door and shone it around the barn. Uno, Dos and Tres squatted in a semicircle and in front of them, cross-legged on the floor sat John. "Hey, buddy. What are you doing up?" I crossed the floor and put my hand on his shoulder. He turned his head to look at me and said "Mmmurrk," pointing to the machines. That was the first time he'd ever tried to speak.

"Mark?" I turned to look at the machines. Big, dumb, waiting.

When I looked back at him whatever light there'd been in his eyes had fled. He just gave me the John grin. And by the smell that rolled off him as I lifted him up he'd need to have a new nappy before I put him back to bed too, go in the shower too maybe. On the way back to the house I realised that John didn't have any way of making light. The torch had been on the wall, as always, and the robots were shut down. Maybe he'd turned the torch on and off when he entered the barn?

By the time I had him cleaned up and in bed I was ready for sleep myself. I dreamt a confused dream about Mark. Where he still lived but no-one else knew, and only I could see him. I hated the dreams that I'd had after mum died where I thought she was alive, until I woke up properly, for weeks. Her death hitting me fresh every morning. I hoped I wasn't going to go through that all over again with Mark.

The next day I trailed after Ramirez as she gave the robots orders. You could program them, or run them in a driver mode or a bit of a mix of both. Looked to me like she was getting to know them as well as teach me about them. She wasn't talkative, over and above giving instructions, and that suited me fine. We spent the day cleaning the soil. Each machine ambling over the ground, scooping up the top several inches at their front, crunching it through some sort of mechanism inside and shitting it back out behind them. I don't know what process the soil got inside them, Ramirez wasn't forthcoming on this - all part of the experiment - but once it'd come out the other side it felt different, smelt different, looked different. They say hope springs eternal but I allowed myself to believe that my desperate gamble was going to pay off. The soil seemed renewed.

When we walked back to the house for dinner, after putting the robots away in the barn, Ramirez told me I'd done good. "You can follow instructions fine. I think I'll be able to hand over to you in a week or so and maybe a few weeks after that

I'll be able to leave you to it. I'll have programmed the robots anyway. And you'll be able to call me if you need advice. Or if they break down."

She went straight to bed after dinner.

I took another beer after putting Pa to bed.

I made sure John was in bed first.

There were several flashes of light in the barn, and nothing to see when I opened it up.

"Do the robots communicate with each other?" I asked Ramirez the next day.

"There's peer to peer messaging so they avoid running into each other and act as each other's data back ups yes."

"Do they… emit light? When they charge up?"

Ramirez stopped concentrating on the control pad and looked at me. "What?"

"Last couple of nights I've noticed flashes of light from the barn," I said.

"And you're only telling me now?"

"Yes, well—"

"Our rivals would love to steal our intellectual property!"

"I… Oh. I hadn't considered that." I scratched my ear and looked over her shoulder at the machines rumbling slowly over a field of grey-brown earth before them and a healthier, redder brown behind.

"Tonight we'll watch together," she said and turned back to her work.

Another day of watching the machines eat and shit soil. Some of it the same soil they'd already done once. The experiment weren't fast. Ramirez let me put all the machines in the barn. "Tomorrow I'll show you how to program them," she said.

We went and cleaned up. Ate the meal Ruth had cooked us and put the children and Pa to bed. Ruth gave me a hard stare when I said that I was going to stay up with Ramirez. Don't know what went through her mind. She looked as though she were going to wait up too, chaperone us. But she only shook her head and climbed the stairs wearily.

"Beer?" I asked Ramirez.

"Sure," she replied.

We took our bottles onto the porch and sat at opposite ends of the swing seat in companionable silence.

"You have good land here," she said eventually.

"Too many damn stones," I countered.

She grinned.

More silence. A bat dive bombed the house. I watched the sky, taking the occasional gulp of beer.

A bright blue flash of light lit up the yard between us and the barn and we were both up and running.

I yanked open the door to the barn when we got there and Ramirez ducked inside just as another bright light split the night. I blinked and the afterimage behind my eyelids had two silhouettes. "Who's there?" I called as I groped for the torch on the wall.

When I switched the light on only Ramirez stood in the centre of the barn. The three robots in a semicircle before her. She panted and her gaze searched the barn - I swung the light around, making sure we could see into all the corners. No-one.

"I'd swear I saw someone," I said.

"You saw it too?"

"Sure, someone else… Wait, it?"

Ramirez gave me a worried look, chewing her lip. "I meant them. You saw them too."

I rubbed my hand across my stubble. "What did you see?"

She shook her head, as if to clear it. "I thought I saw someone. But when you switched the light on, there was no-one there."

"Could have got out somehow?" It sounded weak, even to me. She just shook her head.

We made sure to search the whole barn. But found nothing out of place and certainly no spy. I suggested we call it a night. Ramirez agreed fast, it might have just been the light but her eyes seemed haunted. I wondered what she'd seen. 'It?'

The next day as I watched the machines I said, "Maybe we should keep watch inside the barn?" I tried to read Ramirez's expression out of the corner of my eye.

"Okay," she said eventually.

A whooping, giggling John streaked past us. "Hey," Luke shouted, trying to catch him up. I started forward just as John reached Uno and climbed up him. "Hey!" I echoed Luke. Ramirez brought the machines to a stop. "Those machines are dangerous," she shouted. Between us Luke and I manhandled John, but he thrashed and wailed. Desperate to return to the machines. As we came level with Ramirez she gave us a look. "I mean it," she said. "Those machines are dangerous. They can swallow a boy John's size. Swallow him whole."

John giggled, slippery with sweat he squirmed in my arms. "C'mon, buddy, let's get you inside. And dressed." I gave Ramirez an apologetic look, hoping to convey both that it wasn't my fault and it wouldn't happen again.

"He's getting too much, Matt," Luke said.

"Too big for you to boss around you mean?"

"Since the machines came. He's become excitable. Well, more so. You know?"

Luke sounded worried. If Mark had been here he'd have been able to suggest something. I just nodded. We got John inside. I Left him with Luke and Pa. Went to see Ruth.

"John's too much of a handful for Luke," I said from the kitchen doorway, watching her fill the dishwasher. Baby Emily sat in her armchair gurgling and playing with a bright orange bowl full of beans. She smiled at me and held up a spoon for me to see, the beans spilling out of it and onto the floor.

"We all have to do our bit, Matt." She didn't turn from her task.

"I am." I sighed. "He's going to get worse. He's getting big."

I watched her back stiffen, she paused, holding a plate. "What do you suggest?"

"I don't know, Ruthy, I just don't know."

She shook her head. "Well neither do I." She started filling the dishwasher again.

"Do you think Ma's folks would…"

"Would what? Take him from us? Is that what you want? To send your little brother to live with strangers? He's not an unwanted pet," she rounded on me and I spotted the flush of anger on her. I held up my hands.

"Forget I said anything." I pushed the door open and walked out of the kitchen. The stone cleaves and grows heavier.

John stood at the window, watching the machines, hooting softly to himself. Luke tried to avoid my eye. "Look… Just. Just do your best, yeah?" I told him.

When I returned to the field Ramirez had the machines going again. "Ready to do your job?" she asked. I held my hand out for the control. I wasn't joking about the fields being full of stones. Sharp as shark's teeth.

When we put them in the barn I left Ramirez to it and went and collected two plates of dinner, telling Ruth and the rest that we'd be eating in the barn and standing watch, that we thought there'd been an intruder, but there was nothing to worry about. No-one looked reassured.

Back in the barn, as we ate, I asked Ramirez what the robots ran on.

"Big batteries. Solar, some chemicals from the soil. Atomic," she explained.

"You think the light could actually be coming from them?"

She gave me a long look. "What makes you ask?"

"It's not a camera flash, like you thought. It's not a torch. It looks like the flash you get from an electric source," I watched her face. She gave nothing away.

"So what?"

"What did you see, Ramirez?"

"Same as you. I thought I saw a figure. A man." She looked down and away.

"And?"

She shrugged.

"C'mon, Ramirez. You saw something."

She shook her head. "He didn't look finished," she said, low, quiet.

I put the plate down, food forgotten. "What?"

"It was just a glimpse. But the figure. He seemed wrong. Unfinished. I can't explain it. It was just a flash. Just seeing things that aren't there and not seeing things that are there I suppose." She shook her head again. "Just a foolish fancy." She put her own plate down. "To change the subject back to the power."

"Yeah?"

"You notice that the machines are not fully charged in the mornings? In fact they're getting worse." She reached into the bag she kept the controller in and passed the gizmo to me. I brought up the diagnostics and frowned. She was right each morning the robots weren't at 100%, a little less each day in fact.

I grabbed the two beers I'd brought over with the food and popped their lids and passed one to Ramirez. "What do you think it is?"

"Some sort of malfunction?"

"What if it is the light? Can you see when the batteries drain?"

She took the controller back off me. "I can set it so that the diagnostic will give us hourly figures and… well I'll be." She turned the controller round and I looked at the screen. There was a definite drain around the time we'd seen the flashes. Which were occurring at roughly the same hour each night. We had a few hours to wait yet though, if the pattern held.

Time ticked away slowly. Ramirez wasn't a big talker and neither was I. I wished we'd brought some cards to play or something to pass the time. When I wandered over to the machines Ramirez decided to teach me some more, show me the programming. All in computer code she had to start at first principles - I didn't know code from Greek. It helped pass the time.

She pointed to the time on the controller - any time now would be the drain. She started a diagnostic run through on Uno and the little blue circle span on screen, showing that the machine were thinking.

The bright flash still took me by surprise but I was looking right at it this time and what I saw seared itself on my eyeballs. The shape of a man, standing and then in a blink kneeling, arms thrown out and back, in extreme pain? Skin stripped, muscles bare to the air, mouth in a wide O, eyeballs fizzing, a halo of something surrounding him, blood? But the worst thing of all. I recognised him, I recognised my brother. Mark was trying to come home.

"What the hell?" Ramirez whispered behind me.

"You saw him too?"

"Uh-huh."

Another flash. Like time running backward Mark's form was stripped of more flesh and muscle, his lungs pulsed, heart throbbed, guts shone, and then gone. The third flash was a skeleton, still knelt, arms cruciform, head thrown far back. And darkness.

"Holy shit," Ramirez said. That about summed it up.

We waited in the silence of the night for an unknown time for another flash but it seemed the show was over for tonight.

"It's definitely what's draining the robots," Ramirez confirmed.

I sighed. "It's my brother. Mark. He was in the forces. Boot camp." I made out Ramirez's features in the gloom. Her brows drew together, her forehead wrinkling. "He died."

"You're dead brother is messing with my robots?"

"Well. When you put it like that, it does sound ridiculous."

Ramirez crossed to where I stood, put her hand on my arm. "You have anything stronger than beer?"

I tried to force a smile. "My Pa's an alcoholic. Course we have something stronger than beer."

Back on the swing seat on the porch, a bottle of grain spirit between us, matching glass for glass, Ramirez promised to find out, if she could, what the experimental transportation that killed Mark was. Later, in bed, lying awake, I wondered if I could trust her.

When the troop carriers turned up I guessed it answered the question of trust. Men in military fatigues marched the family out of the house and lined us up in the yard. They buzzed around, filling the yard with men in fatigues being busy. Ramirez looked a little sheepish, threw me an apologetic look, mouthed something, looked like 'it's not my fault.' I blamed her anyway. I didn't see John. Ruth carried Emily on her hip and threw her arm around Luke.

"I need to go find my brother," I said to the soldier who'd lead me to the yard.

He shook his head. "One of ours will bring everyone out," he said.

John's screaming appeared before he did. All activity in the yard ceased, soldiers span toward the sound. He sprinted out of the door, wielding something long in his hand, half-dressed, mouth wide with an ear-splitter. One of the soldiers, spooked, lifted his gun and squeezed off a shot. I screamed, a long no, that would echo forever. The shot took off the top of John's head, splashing brains and blood over the soldier that had appeared in the doorway. I ran forward and tried to catch John. I'd always be trying to catch John. In his hand was the fire engine toy he loved so. His little body was hot in my arms. I couldn't see the yard through tears. I could hear Ruthy wailing. Luke shouting. Army men barking orders. Soldiers threw a tarp over him as they dragged me away.

Ruth and the kids were taken into care; no-one would tell me what happened to Pa. The farm had been locked down; the military boffins investigating what happened to my brother. The company took back its robots and Mark didn't appear again. The army questioned me about the phenomena lots, but of course I knew less than them what it all meant.

Later, at the inquest the soldier would be reprimanded, but he served no jail time for killing my brother. By then the army had fixed its earlier error and I'd been drafted too. Awaiting my turn at the Splitter. The army's new, experimental transport, a matter transmitter. Waiting to be turned into light and flashed across the world at the fastest speed there is. Waiting, and dreading to catch up with my brother Mark. I saw Ramirez again just the once. She'd been drafted too, working tech for the military. She'd seen me. Avoided me. When I asked about her she'd already been transferred to the front line, at her request. The war had started to really hot up. Any day they'd zap me there to kill or be killed.

My Ma had said that the stone of sorrow is sharp, like a shark's tooth, and heavy, like a dead child. And the longer you carry it the more it cleaves to you. If they hadn't prised him from my hands, I could have carried him all day; John wasn't heavy. But even now, the sorrow is still sharp.

One for sorrow,

Two for luck; (or mirth)

Three for a wedding,

Four for death; (or birth)

Five for silver,

Six for gold;

Seven for a secret,

Never to be told;

Eight for heaven,

Nine for hell

And ten for the Devil's own self

THE NIGHT MARKET

HARLAN IS ALREADY fed up with people telling him 'on a good day you can see the whole city from here' because he knows that's a lie. It is not possible to see the whole city as there is a fair amount of it behind the hills. He is also annoyed by this due to the fact that it's not a clear day, it's a filthy night. Plus, working the night market, he is unlikely to ever see a clear day. People are just flapping their lips. How the venues are chosen is obscure but they are communicated via the ranting of street people, the tagging of certain buildings with black graffiti, dead drops and rumour. Tonight the market is on top of a car park, perched on a hill looking out over the valley most of the city is cupped within.

Harlan adjusts the mirrors on his pitch so they shine just so. He has calculated the angles and knows that the mirrors catch the light just right so as to be seen from the entrance. The curious will be lead to his pitch by the sparkling. Each of the stalls are separated by a bit of building material. A tarpaulin here, a bit of plastic blue sheeting there. It gives them the illusion of privacy.

Tonight he is between Kit and Sally, two women he gets along with OK although he'd prefer to be next to a stall that generated more foot traffic than Sally's and less desperation than Kit's. Many bargains are made at the Night Market; life, of a sort, death, love, luck and happiness, of a kind, may be found there. For the tenth time he checks his face in one of his mirrors, remembering to mutter the requisite words not to trigger it. He glances at Sally's pitch, a couple of homeless guys are there trading stuff they've found on the street for a little bit of warmth. Sally is soft hearted and soft headed but tolerable.

So far he's had a slow night. No one seems interested in buying reflections, which is good because he's exhausted. The piece of work he'd done before coming tonight had taken all the little bits & pieces, scraps and favours, bargains and transactions of juice he'd been saving up since winning a pitch. Harlan has worked his way up the strictly enforced hierarchy of the market. From Shadow-runner to Enforcer to Gnomon (he who casts a shadow), but he wants to go further, become one of the 13, the folk that run the market. Not many know who they are, or even if there are, in fact, thirteen of them. At the top is the legendary Papa Cash.

If he performed well for Mr Eustace then he'd get an introduction. That knowledge had come at great expense from Benny the Shark who loaned intelligence at an incredibly stringent interest rate.

He is broken out of his reverie when the light seems to be sucked out of the very air around him. He looks up, and up. Getto stands grinning with two paper cones full of hot potatoes, one of which he thrusts at his friend.

"What you looking so pleased about?" The large man rumbles.

"I think that my third recommendation is on its way," Harlan answers.

Getto's grin widens, then he looks thoughtful. "How d'you know that? No-one knows who the 13 are so no-one knows when they'll give their recommendations."

Sally looks over sharply, coming to the corner of Harlan's stall; she keeps glancing across to the two tramps, one short, one tall, who are still at her stall.

"You're joking, you're going to get another recommendation? That's really not fair, I've been here longer."

Harlan ignores her, she's been jealous of his second recommendation since he got it, she only has the one.

"I just have a feeling that my luck is about to change," Harlan says popping a hot chip in his mouth.

"You been purchasing at Mr Eustace's stall then?" Getto says as Sally goes to deal with a customer.

"Mr Eustace?" Harlan squeaks, turning it into a "ho-ho-hot" while flapping his hand in front of his mouth.

Getto looks momentarily concerned then continues "Yeah, the luck guy"

Harlan then remembers that someone had said that Eustace dealt in luck.

"No, no just a feeling I've got."

"Hey Harlan, have I told you about Penny, nineteen?" Getto says pulling out the well-thumbed magazine he seemed to carry everywhere and flips it open to a picture of a naked girl with scared eyes. Harlan sighs as his eyes slip from the centrefold to his friend's meaty arm and the black raven of the enforcers tattooed there. He rubs absently at the same tattoo on his own arm. Life as an enforcer had been easier.

***

Kit deals in time, buying and selling it with those who find they either have time on their hands or need a few more seconds, minutes or hours. Her stall has timepieces of all types and designs, each holding those few precious moments that may come in handy on a rainy day. Or they are waiting patiently to be filled. She doesn't mind being next to Harlan. He is decent enough for a bald, short, ugly man. She knows he's had two recommendations and is desperate for the third and so does what she can to stay in his good books. You never know when you'll need a favour from someone well placed.

Her hand flashes out like a striking snake to capture the bony wrist of someone reaching out towards one of her clocks, a particular gaudy one carved out of volcanic rock from some ghastly down market holiday resort.

"Look no touch!" she says, looking into the eyes of the man whose face is muffled in a red woollen scarf. Dressed in a faded tuxedo with long tails is an older gentleman, thin, with long white hair yellowed at the ends, he stares pointedly at Kit's hand on his arm which she belatedly drops. "Mr Eustace."

"Apologies," he says and puts a pack of playing cards on the plank resting on two boxes that is acting as her counter tonight. "Can we trade?"

They spend a few minutes bargaining. Eustace seems to be in a hurry but Kit has ceased to keep track of such things as she has all the time in the world. When he leaves she has a smidgeon of good luck, he's left with several minutes of extra time. They are both happy.

She'd be happier if she had just one recommendation. She knew Harlan had two, hell even Sally had one. No-one could deal outside the city unless they had three recommendations, those that earn the favour of the 13, the ones that receive the black velvet seal, the ones they call 'honourable cousin'. She isn't jealous like Sally, well not quite as jealous, nor would she bad mouth Harlan behind his back like Sally. She's just not that two faced. Perhaps that means she's not cut out to be a 'mover and shaker' in the Night Market's hierarchy?

***

Harlan welcomes Mr Eustace to his stall.

"Honourable cousin."

"Harlan."

Getto takes the hint of Harlan's rapidly shooing motions and goes off to talk to another of his friends.

"So..."

"Drink, Mr Eustace?"

The old man shakes his head. Harlan is at a loss and waits patiently. Mr Eustace stares at him, his eyes narrow.

"What do you want Harlan?"

"Want?"

"Yes, why did you want to see me?"

"Oh er, well, you see, it's um, delicate," Harlan starts and immediately falls into silence as Eustace holds his hand up.

"This *is* a professional matter isn't it?"

Harlan blinks rapidly, "Professional, yes er, totally."

Eustace sighs. "Proceed."

Harlan goes through his spiel. "Mr Eustace," he begins, "I have an offer for you, an unsurpassed offer, a three dimensional image, of the finest craftsmanship. In return I need a bit of luck, you see I'm after a third recommendation, I wish to get the black seal." He can see Eustace's eyes narrowing.

"Couldn't you just have come to my stall?"

"Oh, er, well yes, I could have done that, but here is more private, and you can do the formalities here, now."

"Ok, let's talk trade."

Harlan spots that Sally has edged closer, trying to overhear the conversation. "Perhaps if we can be a little circumspect?"

Their voices fall to a whisper. A few minutes later they shake hands. Eustace chews the end of his long, nicotine yellow moustache.

"Later," he says and immediately turns and walks off.

Harlan mops his face with a handkerchief. He checks the traps. Got him! He thinks. He glances at Sally's stall but she's deep in conversation with the tramps. Harlan gets to work, in the shadowy interior of his stall.

***

IT TAKES A while, but eventually all the stored energy, all the planning, all the work pays off. Mr Eustace, the second Mr

Eustace, stands at the back of Harlan's stall. Harlan wraps a scarlet scarf around the image's face and opens a way to behind the stall. "You know what to do?" The image nods once then walks out into the narrow corridor between stalls, turns into the main 'street' and disappears into the crowd. Now all Harlan can do is wait. He waves a runner over and sends for a hot drink. He notes the two tramps leaving Sally's stall. The taller of the two walks towards the exit of the market, the short one towards the centre.

***

THE SCREAMS START about five minutes later. They startle Harlan from his reverie. He is standing looking into one of the deactivated mirrors; most of the ones on the stall are out of juice now. He is whispering to himself "Honourable cousin, Honourable... cousin, *Honourable* cousin." His head whips round when the first scream pierces the air. There is a general movement in the crowd towards the middle of the market. Where the oldest, most connected, honourable cousins of the market ply their trade. The Gnomon cannot move from their pitches, not whilst there are customers, not if they want to retain their stock.

A runner sprints by and Harlan manages to snag him by the collar bringing him up short with an 'erk' and splutter.

"What's happening?" he asks the boy.

"Someone has killed Mr Eustace," the boy says. Harlan lets go of the boy instantly, who runs off. Harlan immediately pops next door.

"Kit, can I purchase an hour off you? I'll owe you one."

Kit looks shrewdly at him, glances at the general hubbub, and nods wordlessly handing him an old brass ship's clock which he gratefully receives. She starts thinking about what she can get from Harlan as a favour returned.

Back at his own stall he paces back and forth, barely noticing the customers.

The hand that falls on his shoulder stops him dead in his tracks.

He looks up into Getto's face. His friend is no longer grinning.

"He was last seen at your stall," the big man says.

"Yes, that's er possible," Harlan replies, trying not to look guilty.

"You have until the sun comes up to prove it wasn't you," Getto says releasing him. "But the Ravens will gather at dawn."

Harlan gulps. An unkindness of Ravens. He knows what that means.

"My pitch?"

"Closed."

Harlan nods, he breaks his pitch down with practiced hands and passes the resultant large bundle to the enforcer who lifts it easily with one hand, swings it across his back, and then stalks off towards the centre of the market. He checks on the spell holding the image together, squares his shoulders and marches across the market, aware of all the eyes on him, the runners and the Gnomon curious and accusing.

***

THE OBVIOUS PLACE to start is at Mr Eustace's stall where he finds that it has been overturned; the carrion pickers have snatched their trophies already. Eustace lies where he has fallen, surrounded by a deck of cards splashed with his blood. It is obvious that the gaping hole in his chest is what's killed him. Harlan examines the wound, taking out his flashlight and shining it in there. Looks like a jagged weapon did this. His flashlight picks out something glittering in the wound - silvered glass. Oh that's bad, very sloppy. He picks it out and pockets it.

The stall on the left is run by an elderly Japanese man. Harlan is not surprised that these prime pitches are run by the oldest of the Gnomon. He is surprised that the Japanese man cannot speak much English.

"Did you see anything?" Harlan asks.

"Wha?" the old man answers.

"At the stall, did you see anyone, anything?"

"Wha?"

Harlan suspects that his chain is being yanked and that the language thing is an act.

"You," he says pointing to the old man, "see," he says pointing to his eyes, "anything," lost for a mime he just points to the stall.

"Wha?"

Harlan doesn't purchase any of the stall's netsuke affection charms.

The stall on the other side houses another old timer. Veronica, a tough old bird that Harlan knows. She trades in a less salubrious emotion. She appears to be in a foul mood, helped no doubt by the copious amounts of sour whiskey she's been drinking.

"Whaddya want?"

"Did you see anything?"

"Saw double for a bit, seemed to have got over that now."

"Double? As in two Mr Eustaces?"

"Yup."

"What happened?"

"They stood toe to toe looking at each other and moving like checking that the person in the mirror isn't someone else on the other side, you know? Then the one reaches out to the other, they shake hands, the red scarf flutters to the floor. Then I get a customer. In the middle of the consultation I hear a scream, and then Eustace is on the floor. Dead."

"Was there anyone else that came to his stall, before or after the man in the red scarf?"

"Nossir." Veronica scratches at her chin, sucks on her teeth and blows air out her nostrils. "Well mebbe one man, short like you but not as well dressed. Furtive. Didn't stop none, came, looked, moved on, didn't see where he went."

"Before or after?"

"Before some." Veronica takes a large swig out of the bottle she's holding. "Dammit, that old bastard owed me."

Harlan thanks the old woman and goes back to Eustace's stall.

***

THE TWO RAVENS that are now guarding the stall are unknown to Harlan. One blocks him as he tries to enter. He wonders if he should push it but decides that he should save any confrontations for later. He looks into the heart of the market, at a stall shrouded in black with all sorts of skulls hanging on it; from sparrows to sloths, hummingbirds to humans. He shudders. There is nothing for it, only really one place to go. He swallows his fear.

***

THE CORPULENT MAN looks at Harlan entering his pitch, "Harlan, this is a nice surprise, such an enjoyable surprise, I mean it, it is a wonder and it's so pleasant to see you again so soon. You have come with my payment, my recompense?" Full jowls hang down that wobble as he speaks, he is sweating profusely. There is a plate of ribs in front of him. He wipes his fingers on a napkin and gestures Harlan inside. There are a couple of customers who take one look at Harlan, at the Raven tattoo, and leave.

"Er, no, Benny, I haven't, I, well, I'd like to take out another loan."

"Another loan? An additional lending? Is that wise Harlan, is that prudent?"

"I'm good for it, you know that."

"You mistake me Harlan. Is that wise Harlan, is it sensible, for me?"

Harlan looks surprised.

Benny wipes his mouth and stands up, he is not a tall man but he is a wide man and his bulk is imposing.

"I hear that the Ravens are gathering at dawn, congregating."

Harlan should have known.

"A little bird tells me that you are in trouble, misfortune." Benny flutters his fingers rubbing them against his thumbs vigorously. "This information will cost you extra, additional."

Harlan winces, but nods. "Agreed."

"Splendid. Marvellous. Sit, be seated." Benny sits himself, takes up a rib and has a tiny delicate bite from it. "Entrails?"

"Er, no thank you, I've eaten."

Benny looks at him to make sure he's joking and then laughs perfunctorily. He takes further bites. Small, dainty, pecking at the food.

"No, you're right, mmm you're correct. A subtler form is called for. Sortilege perhaps. If it is one of us, one of the Gnomon, they'll be protected against scrying, secured and safe." Between words he takes bites from the ribs.

Harlan nods, he has sworn that oath himself. "But, in a way, that's an answer too."

"Indeed, certainly." Benny wipes his mouth. Each of the ribs is picked clean. "Cleromancy," he says, picking up the bones and fanning them between his fingers. "Your question?"

Harlan is familiar with the rules of this game since he played is so recently. A yes/no answer. Traditionally three questions.

"Did the image do it?"

Benny flicks his hands and the bones fall into a jumble "No."

"Did a customer do it?"

Benny gathers the bones, fans them then flicks his hands again "Yes."

Harlan's last question is now not needed. Or maybe, "Were they paid to do it?"

Sweep, fan, flick "Yes."

"We shall settle up, pay the balance before dawn yes?" Benny sweeps the plate and the bones from the table.

"Yes, Benny, I will pay before dawn." Harlan looks at his watch, he only has an hour. He pats his pocket and the bulk of the ship's clock reassures him. He takes it out and smashes it onto the floor. Now he has two hours.

"I do so hope you'll tidy that, make it neat? Hmmm?" Benny says, staring pointedly at the mess of glass and cogs. Sheepishly, Harlan takes out his handkerchief and brushes it up.

***

There is a heavy smell of incense barely covering a more troublesome odour. Harlan doesn't want to think what's bubbling away in the cauldron and waits patiently behind a woman who is finishing up her bargain with the small, bespectacled man who looks like a librarian sat behind the counter. Whatever the bargain, the member of the public hefts what is obviously a heavy sports bag, which bulges alarmingly, onto the counter. The man in glasses lifts, with some difficulty, a very large leather bound book onto the counter and opens it. The woman signs and immediately turns around and leaves looking grim.

"Harlan."

"Honourable cousin."

"Client confidentiality?"

"What? How did you… ?"

The small man pushes his wire rimmed glasses up his nose and smiles. "Really Harlan. You have to ask?"

"Well er, no, no I guess not. But well, can't you cut me a break? For old times' sake?"

The man steeples his fingers touching them to his lips. "I'm afraid not Harlan." They stare at each other for a beat or two. Harlan is just opening his mouth to say something when the man behind the counter speaks.

"Could you just keep an eye on the stall whilst I pop out a second?" The man's eyes flick down to the ledger on the counter for a split second and then he gets up and goes out.

Harlan reads upside down the list of people who had bought a death tonight and sees Sally's name there. She appears to have bought the death of someone called 'Two Coats'.

***

It doesn't take much asking around to find that Two Coats was a tramp, the short man who'd been at Sally's pitch earlier. Apparently she'd traded a service off him. In return for food and warmth, he'd killed the old man. She'd then paid for him to have an accident. Harlan passes all this info on to Getto.

"Why d'you do it Sal?" Getto asks when they come to take her away.

She glares at him, "I didn't do nothing." She spots Harlan standing watching, "It's not fair," she screeches at him. "I've been here longer, my stuff has a better appeal so I should get the recommendations, not you, never you!"

Getto shakes his head. "One Gnomon killing another? It's not unknown. But it's usually done in a more intelligent way."

"I never killed anyone!" she shouts as she's taken away. "No-one, d'you hear me?"

Getto pats Harlan on the back, a meaty slap. "I knew it wasn't you but the accused has to clear his own name, you understand, you've been there."

Harlan nods. "I owe you a drink."

As Harlan puts his stall back up, a runner passes him a message. Intriguing. A rendezvous when the Market closes, with whom, for what?

***

Kit is happy that tonight she got her first recommendation.

Benny is happy to have a number of reflections.

Getto is happy that the peace has been kept, the 13 untroubled, no new feuds have started.

***

Later, as the Night Market is broken down, Harlan walks into the shadowed alley between the car park and the ice rink it sits next to. An old man hides in the gloom.

"Papa Cash thanks you."

Harlan raises his eyebrows. "You?"

"Me."

"How did you do it?"

"The image was obviously the one that was killed, I just called in a few favours, it was easy enough to frame Sally since the ledger keeper was paid to look the other way. I hope the Black Seal is worth your time and expense, Harlan. Perhaps we'll do business again sometime?" Mr Eustace passes the Black Seal to Harlan who rubs his fingers over it.

"I'm glad to help, although I'm not sure what it is I've just done exactly."

"You have given me freedom."

"I don't understand."

"Don't you? The 13 must remain anonymous. I congratulate you for finding out. We could have eliminated you, but that would have been a waste, far better to groom you and eliminate some other, well how do I put this delicately, dead weight. Now I will move on, the 13 are active in other cities you know. Farewell Harlan, I wish you well."

Harlan watches the old man walk out of the alley and into a waiting black car with tinted windows. This is big, much bigger than him. He rubs his fingers over the seal again. He has a sudden thought. But he knows about Eustace, nothing has been solved. He thinks about Eustace's last words to him, as long as he continues to be useful, he thinks. He strokes the Black Seal "Honourable Cousin," he says softly.

One for sorrow,

Two for luck; (or mirth)

Three for a wedding,

Four for death; (or birth)

Five for silver,

Six for gold;

Seven for a secret,

Never to be told;

Eight for heaven,

Nine for hell

And ten for the Devil's own self

MARRIED IN BLUE

NONE OF US had seen a horse that colour. Nor a rider like that neither. Red and the rider upon it dressed all in silver with a great sword. A lifetime would not be enough for the men of the village to earn the money for armour such as that. Not even all of them together. Da was first to speak to him.

"Stable for your horse, good sir?"

Honest. What he'd say to any other visitor. Those with horses anyway. That's how he made his money. Taking in horses for the inn. The stranger moved slowly, majestically. His face unreadable behind the full visor of his helm. He dismounted gracefully and threw the reins to my father, and a small velvet bag full of golden coins. I picked them up. Perhaps that's when he first noticed me?

He stayed at the inn of course, nowhere else in the village to stay. "I'm waiting for someone," is all he said. Several of us sneaked glances at him, contriving to be in the common room. My job, as a serving wench, gave me legitimacy. I caught his eye alright. I can tell.

The next day he came to breakfast, still in his shiny suit but without the helm. He was big boned, not really handsome, but not ugly neither. Long red hair. Calm, placid face. He seemed to be kicking his heels waiting for whoever. I started chatting with him, just to pass the time.

"They say there's trouble at the border. That the King's army are mobilising. That there's a possibility of invasion." He just stared at me. I kept trying. "Is that where you're headed?"

"Where?"

"The army? The border?"

"Possibly. I must await the others."

Then things got busy and I didn't speak to him again during my shift. The next day there was another stranger in town, just passing through, his horse had shed a shoe and Da was fixing it. While Da worked I overheard some of their conversation.

"Can't outrun it if you is set on stayin' here," he said, with many a look down the road.

Da grunted, taking the horse's leg's weight. "Can't outrun war none anyways."

"Nor the sickness that follows after," the stranger said, spitting to one side. I was about to ask him about the sickness when I was called to work. I asked the man in the shiny suit instead.

"I hear there is a sickness coming?"

He turned his great bovine face to me then, staring at me with his mournful eyes. "Not just a sickness," he said, looking as though he knew something, maybe too much. His jaw tightened. "Where did you hear this news, girl?"

"In the stable, a stranger, and it's Saffie."

He paused momentarily in the act of rising to his feet. When he was standing he glanced at me. His deep eyes unfathomable. "What's Saffie?"

"My name, sir."

He nodded, as if I'd just confirmed something he had, until then, suspected. Without another word, or looking back, he strode to the stables. I longed to follow him but had work to do. In less than an hour he was back at his place. Still waiting, but I fancied a little more impatiently.

The next day men came from the other direction. They filled the inn with tall tales of marching armies, of razed villages, of the sickness that follows, of the armies gathering up all the food. They ate ravenously, gambled foolishly, partied wantonly and left sheepishly. He sat like a deity awaiting worship throughout. He used my name. I went to him for protection from the drunken revellers. When things got too raucous he took me to his room. Things … well they just happened from there. He was massively scarred, hugely muscled and the gentlest lover I've ever had.

For the next few weeks the news from outside the village got worse and worse and yet the battles and armies seemed to be forever elsewhere. We seemed blessed. My paramour's name was as mysterious to me as the rest of him. Oh I asked, many times. Was it a sign of love that he didn't tell me? Or was it a sign that he did not love me? No traveller who came to town stayed long.

It came as a great surprise when one day, nestled into his shoulder, dozing after lovemaking, he said "I have asked your father for your hand." It was as though he had thrown a bucket of cold water on me, I sat up straight.

"What?"

He just gazed at me with those depthless eyes. I had never seen him smile, nor display anything but stoicism. "Does this not please you?" he asked.

He had never expressed love, or even affection, he had never become angry with me, or exhibited any emotion. I had begun to think he was one of those men that couldn't, although I could make him feel lust, there was nothing wrong with his body, that part of his body anyway. We batted the idea around for a bit, well at least I did most of the talking. In the end, although I'm not sure why, I said yes. He put his armour away and joined Da in the stables, seemed he knew how to smith. I was going to marry the blacksmith. His name became Smith.

The news from the rest of the kingdom didn't change. Battles were fought, people became ill, people starved, people died. Some refugees came to our town, but they didn't stay long. The inn, once a bustling hub for travellers, became sadly forlorn. Like a dog awaiting a master who would never return.

A week or so later I was to be married, in my mother's beautiful blue dress that Da had been saving all these years. Smith cared every day for his large red horse. He paid it more attention than he paid me. "Are you still waiting?" I asked him.

"If they come it will all change." It was the same answer he gave the last three times I had asked him this question. Today he stared at me. "Do you want them to come?" It was not expected. I played for time. "Who are they?"

"Family, of sorts, friends, sometimes, obligations."

"Family and friends should be at the wedding," I said and immediately regretted it. He nodded. A shadow of an expression crossed his face, like a high, fast cloud on a sunny day. Later I saw him leave the inn with a well-worn leather sack I had never seen before. I followed him, at a distance, so he didn't see. In the woods on the edge of town he released three black and white birds that took to the trees and clacked in outraged voices. His shoulders seemed a little slumped when he turned to return to town. I had to run to stay out of sight. I burned to ask him, but was ashamed of following him and a little afraid too.

That evening, as storm clouds gathered and a dry, irritating wind blew into the village, a small round woman on a scabby white horse arrived. The small woman was syphilitic, but she had gold. The horse was stabled, but I could see its state hurt Da inside.

As soon as the woman entered the inn she took a place at the table Smith habitually occupied. I expected my paramour to object. As usual he displayed no emotion. He asked for the inn to be emptied, to speak to this stranger alone. I sneaked into a position where I could listen, but they whispered and I only gathered a few phrases and words: 'The four… cannot marry… it comes… war… death.' I focused on the words 'cannot marry' and examined what I felt about that and was surprised to feel relief mixed in with outrage, anger and sadness. I squirmed out of hiding to go to tell Da.

My way was blocked by a massive coal black horse, and sat upon it a man dressed all in black, with a raggedly woollen cloak that flapped a little in the wind, sounding a little like a bird's wing. Da was dwarfed holding its reins. The large man dismounted and spared me not a glance as he strode over to the inn, threw open the door and, with a cry of welcome, rolled in. Friend or family? I wondered. I couldn't hear what was shouted as the air was split by thunder.

I hurried across to Da. "Da, I've heard them speaking." He gave me a sharp glance. "Accidentally. The lady on the white horse? She said that Smith couldn't marry me." Da opened his mouth to answer and was interrupted by a loud whinny as an ashen grey horse cantered down the road towards us and the heavens opened. Hailstones like arrowheads careened off every surface. The woman on the pale grey horse hunched over, holding a hand above her head, flinching at each slap of hail. She was the thinnest woman I had ever seen, her skin, I swear this is true, was yellow. Another horse for the stable, another piece of gold for Da, another guest for the inn. She didn't pass any pleasantries; she seemed to know where she was going.

When the horse was seen to I started again. "But he did say it." Da looked askance at me. "Let's see what Smith says. When he comes over. When the storm has passed. Help me get the barn secure."

We worked like nothing was wrong, fast and efficient, like always. I wondered why the rest of the village was in darkness, why no candles burned away the gloom in any of the windows I could see.

I was patting the pale horse and giving it a handful of oats when Smith came in. He was still expressionless, although his eyes narrowed a little when he saw the horses. They each snorted and grinned in greeting. "I must leave," he eventually said. I was torn inside; a fat tear escaped my eye and slalomed down my face. "But before I do so I will honour you. Fetch your dress."

Everything happened in a whirr, I had no maid of honour,

no maids at all, there were no guests, no family, friends, fellow villagers. The buildings were deserted. There was just me and Da and once he handed me over to my soon to be husband and his brother? Friend? Colleague? The one performing the ceremony. I never saw him again. The storm was titanic, Earth shattering, and continuous. When I said "I do." I could hardly hear myself. When we kissed I was surprised that he was in his armour. How could I not have noticed that? When we broke apart he put his hand on my belly and kissed my forehead. "I must go."

His sword was across his back, under his arm his cavernous helm. I watched him walk across the church and out of the door. The four horses stood ready. My husband was going to work.

One for sorrow,

Two for luck; (or mirth)

Three for a wedding,

Four for death; (or birth)

Five for silver,

Six for gold;

Seven for a secret,

Never to be told;

Eight for heaven,

Nine for hell

And ten for the Devil's own self

LE SACRE DU PRINTEMPS

THE CLOCKWORK RELIQUARY is a masterpiece. Ebony with brass cogs and sepia glass cradling delicate bones that sit on a cushion of grey dust. A brass key thrusts from its workings.

"What's it for?" the Composer asks.

The shop assistant perks up at the prospect of a possible customer. "It is inspiration distilled. The finger bones of Rossini, the dust of Handel."

The composer scratches at the glass, a coating of dust curling slowly from under his perfectly manicured nails.

He has written nothing for weeks. His previous ballet was such a hit the demons of success had crept into his mind and stolen his creativity. He has to have it. Once he holds its weight in his delicate musician's hands he has to use it, but in order to use it he needs tuition.

"How does it work?"

The shop assistant shrugs. The composer attempts to turn the key but it is stiff, so stiff he is afraid of applying too much pressure. He may break it, or worse cut his fingers. Such a thing of beauty: so intricate, so weighty, so marvellous. He hasn't the first idea how it could work but he has a sudden faint inkling of what it could do. It could be the genesis of his next work. He glances at the shop assistant and winces slightly as he sees the acquisitive look she gives him, he knows, and it now appears that she knows, that he is going to buy it. Now it is just a matter of price.

He turns it over. On the bottom is etched a tiny signature. *Milo Grün*

The name means nothing yet. He will have to spend some more money in order to find out who Herr Grün is and where he can be found. He is already planning his search, hiring a specialist perhaps, as he half-heartedly bargains with the shop assistant. They both know that he wants it with an intense and sudden desire, but he is determined to not pay the ridiculous figure she suggests. After twenty minutes or so of haggling he leaves feeling, although not totally successful and a lot poorer, fulfilled in his sudden desire to own the reliquary. He doesn't examine this need too closely, he just knows that this is what he's been looking for; this will make or break him.

It takes him a month, and another substantial fee he can barely afford, to find out that Milo Grün is a reclusive Swiss inventor who lives in Clarens. And yet he knows, if he can just get the reliquary to work, he will make his money back ten times over.

Clarens is only a few days travel, maybe less if he eschews some comfort. He makes his plans in haste and assures his manager, and his wife, that he will return imminently and in triumph. Clarens is a destination other great composers have visited in the past.

"It is there," he tells his manager, "that I will find the proper inspiration to create this piece that my soul is burning for. It will be my greatest work." Of course he says nothing about the reliquary, wrapped with immense care in his luggage. The true reason he travels, it is the compass for his inspiration.

When the composer arrives in the small lakeside town, he rushes to the small shop owned by Herr Grün. The little brass bell above the door tinkles to signal his arrival. He stands expectantly as he can hear bustling and noises of woodworking coming from a curtained off room behind the little counter. He glances around the varied clockwork mechanisms, at a loss as to the purpose of most of them. A wan shaft of sunlight illuminates the counter and the nearest machines but the room has over-stacked shelves full of possible wonders in a thousand different materials, redolent of pine and sawdust, rare perfumes and oil, delicate golden toys sit next to baroque brass gewgaws. The composer has no eyes for these though. He places the reliquary on the counter and bends to unwrap it. As he does so the noises in the next room stop and the curtain is moved aside with slow inevitability.

The white-haired man who comes through the curtain, seemingly with no small amount of reluctance, greets him gruffly. His glance falls naturally to the reliquary and he stops still, eyes twinkling, seemingly holding his breath for a few seconds.

"You have brought The Muse back to me."

"The Muse?"

"One of them, yes. I captured it. Bent it to my will. I don't think it has ever forgiven me. I was sad to see it go, but it is a one-time only affair. Use it and pass it on." He pauses, and looks the composer in the eye. "You could use it though. Anyone could. It will appear for you, if you use the reliquary correctly. It will take whatever form is required."

"Tell me. Tell me everything!"

The composer leaves with precise instructions on how to use the reliquary. He will not wait to summon his inspiration. He hurries to find somewhere to stay that has a music room, that is remote but with easy travel to Clarens. After hiring an agent he finds the perfect chalet. A small log-built four room affair, out of the way, with a piano.

***

THE CLOCKWORK WHIRRS. He watches the coloured light play

across the wall of his hired villa as he waits for the Muse to come. His breathless anticipation turns to impatience, turns to boredom, turns to anger as the hours pass and he steadily works his way through a bottle of wine. He determines to take the reliquary back to Herr Grün's in the morning. As his disgust reaches its peak and he reaches the bottom of the bottle there is a knock at the front door.

Opening the door wide and using it to steady his posture the composer flinches from the biting cold wind that leaps inside. Standing in the doorway, in flawless evening wear, is a handsome young man. He seems immune to the cold and has no obvious means of transportation to the isolated villa.

"Who are you?" the composer says a little too loudly.

"You called?" the visitor says, his voice melted honey.

The composer stares at this vision for a few seconds before he remembers himself.

"I, er, yes, come in, come in." He bustles the visitor into the music room, marvelling at the poetic movements of the Muse as he walks.

"Would you like a drink? Something warm perhaps?" He is unable to tear his gaze from the unblemished skin of the Muse. There is a sense of artificiality about him that the composer cannot place and he glances at the piano, thinking of ivory and ebony.

Seeing where the composer is looking, the Muse says, "play it for me."

The composer sits at the piano and nervously does a few hand exercises to warm up. He glances at the Muse, who may as well be a statue for all the expression on his face. He shudders then closes his eyes and begins to play his composition, the one he has sweated over, wept over, the one his reputation hangs on.

Once the first few bars are out of the way and he has relaxed a little he feels the music move him. He puts everything into this performance, thinking this is the inspiration he is receiving from the Muse. He hasn't played like this for years, simultaneously in command and afraid of what his audience will feel, his very special audience of one. He feels as though his old piano master is standing behind him with the wooden rule he would occasionally slam on his hands if he made a mistake. That was always his greatest fear, not that he disappointed the old man, but that the rule would damage his hands. He loses himself in the piece. He cannot say if he has played for minutes or hours when the final bars slowly fade into silence. He followed his vague unstructured plan and yet he has added so much. When it finishes, he wipes his brow and dares to look for approval.

The Muse lifts its lip in a sneer. Its face betrays the utter contempt it feels for the piece. The composer grinds his teeth as he takes a massive breath, as though surfacing from a deep dive. His hands clench and there is a bang and a sudden discordant note from the piano as he leaps up and flies across the room. A blind, all-consuming rage takes him. He sees the sneer, just the sneer taking up his whole vision and starts punching it. He can't stop. Hitting. Punching. Beating. Until the Muse's face is bloodied pulp.

The mist leaves his eyes. He is straddled across the Muse's chest, which no longer moves. No heart beats below him. The last bubbling breaths had been a lifetime ago.

He looks down at his throbbing hands. He has always looked after his hands; as a composer he needed to look after his hands. They are ruined now. Pain screams from him, jagged and hot, growing stronger as the adrenalin starts to wear off. Fragments of bone show through broken skin, where his knuckles grazed the Muse's teeth. More than one finger is bent and broken. His feels the blood drain from his face and his muscles go slack. His mind slips past what this will mean. He can't grasp it. He has destroyed his hands, his livelihood, his future.

He has killed someone.

***

Herr Grün does not look surprised, but his eyes are full of pity to see the composer returning to his shop, holding his once beautiful hands in front of him, swollen and misshapen. The composer hadn't known where to turn. He had come straight to the man who had set him on this path. "It is always thus," the old man tells him. "Go home, sleep. It is part of the process. You will not be arrested, you will not be maimed, you will wake inspired. Go home, go home."

This last as he pushes the composer out of his door. There is no struggling.

The composer avoids the music room, glad he had made sure he was alone in the house before he summoned the Muse. His steps are heavy, his movement lethargic. He trudges straight to the bedroom, collapses across the bed and sleeps, dreamlessly, soundly, deeply.

When the sun breaks through the half closed curtain the composer stirs. His first thought as he awakes is that he should not have drunk so much. His closed eyes give him a sense of red that remind him of the wine, of the spilled blood... He opens his eyes, fully awake and stares disbelievingly at his hands which are whole, unblemished, undamaged. Wonderingly, he rushes into the music room.

There is no body, no sign of violence. No sign of the reliquary, which had sat on top of the piano. A great weight has been lifted from him. He goes and throws open the shutters, glad to see the sun is shining. He utters a great sigh and takes a deep breath of the fresh spring air. He goes straight to the piano and starts to play.

What starts to come alive beneath his fingers is dissonant, wild, savage even. He imagines strangled brass and fluttering woodwind as his fingers pluck the melody from some space newly available to him. His fingers have a life of their own as they stab and bash at the piano keys. He can barely keep up as a well of repressed creative energy erupts from within. One hand continues to play, a path from inner ear and imagination direct to the piano, whilst the other jerkily scrapes the score onto paper. The music possesses him, draining out of his fingers in great arterial spurts of noise. He is enchanted, enraptured, enthralled. This, this right here, was why he lived, why he composed. When he beats the final few notes from the tortured instrument he is drained and listless. But when he reads the score it reinvigorates him. He laughs; he leaps to his feet and paces: he burns to share this.

***

They have taken a lot of persuasion. Every single person involved was initially sceptical; his manager, the conductor and choreographers, even the ballet dancers. However it was to be in Paris, after many hundreds of hours of practice, that the music would finally be brought to life in the theatre. The cast nervously take in the packed house. They reassure each other, whisper to each other that he is a great composer. When the lights go down and the music starts the initial hush is broken by murmurs and the performers can see the crowd looking at each other. Born from violence, the music goes straight to the hearts of the audience and each takes their measure. It isn't long before hisses and boos echo around the auditorium. Other audience members try to defend the work, calling for silence. Tempers flare, fists start to fly. It is a scandal. It is a riot.

It is an outstanding milestone in music.

After, he is struck with a deeply worrying malaise, spiritual in nature but manifesting in dark lassitude and overall weakness. The composer is reminded of when his mother took him to see *The Pathetique*, in memory of Tchaikovsky, who had suddenly been carried off by cholera. He asks his manager to tell people he has the disease, perhaps caught from the oysters he is known to enjoy?

In winter, whilst convalescing, the composer walks the lake once more. Herr Grün's workshop is boarded up. The sign, once bright, is now shabby with flaking paint, the door, although nailed shut, is bowed with age, and rust grows like lichen on the exposed window brackets. When the composer asks around no-one can remember a Herr Grün, they tell him the old shop has been closed for years. The villa he hired is still there and the owner tells him he could have it for spring again, for the same price. So he knows he didn't dream the entire time he was here. The reliquary though, as promised, was a one-time only affair. However the sacrifice, if such it was, seemed to have worked. Igor Fyodorovich Stravinsky isn't sure it was all worth it. He still has nightmares about his hands.

***

WHEN THE RITE of Spring premièred in Paris in 1913 it sparked a riot. It has since been considered one of the most influential pieces of music of the 20th Century.

ACROSS THE BORDER

Her name's Melinda, caught between child and teenager. Outside in all weathers in red raincoat and yellow wellies, to escape the regime of the house by the sea. She is a bright flash across the bleak landscape, red and yellow against the heather, the bracken, the gorse.

His name's John, reduced to observer, silent watcher of future history unfolding. He walks along the border near the house by the sea. He's accompanied by his ghost of a dog, all white mist and frivolity. The house by the sea has been a constant in his life for years now. He has not got used to it. It is on the border. That arbitrary line, created by long dead cartographers, does little to obscure his view, or hinder his wild walks. The house stands sentinel, one side facing the sea to the east, one side facing north, nominally another country, one south, a previous home, and one west, the direction he always approaches from. It is habit, ingrained, immutable.

The house is grey, squat and ugly, a funny kink on one side showing a botched extension, a yearning to expand north. It has always seemed changeless, presenting the same unforgiving face to him, but today there is another car in the drive. The dour house lit up as if for a festival. He sees that Melinda stalks the barren hills nevertheless; he thinks today she scowls more. She doesn't see him. She never sees him.

He draws close, to hear her monologue.

"Stupid. Why does he have to move in? Stupid accent. Stupid car. Stupid southerner."

He leaves her to her own devices. The festivity an intrusion onto childish grief. Until he is drawn across the border again.

As he circumnavigates the house, watching for Melinda, he sees the north side proudly exhibiting the blue and white, a massive 'YES' pasted to one window. The south side brandishes the red, white and blue and declares 'No Thanks!'

A flash of red amongst the grey old men of the standing stones leads him to her. She is lecturing a snail.

"If we get freedom you'll live in a different country, with all the change that will bring. Do what your heart tells you but listen to your head too. That's what they're saying. If we get freedom she'll marry him. I'll have to change my name. I don't want to change my name."

John is saddened at this intimation of childhood's end. In Mandarin, a language he'd once learned a bit of, for fun, to ask someone's name you said 'you are what name?' - 'Ni jiao shen me ming zi?' Did that mean that if you changed your name, you changed your entire identity? You are what name? The seagull's cries bring him back to the present, his gaze drawn once again to the house by the sea. An uncomfortable view.

He is drawn back to the house. To the argument.

"She's your daughter!"

"I would have hoped you'd think of her as yours too by now." His wife is annoyed, snarling, hurt.

"So you want me to punish her? Won't that make her hate me more?"

"John – "

"For fuck's sake woman, I'm not John and I'd appreciate it if you didn't bring him up in every fucking argument. I can't replace him, she'll never accept me."

John drifts away again, knowing that he will be drawn back. Tomorrow and the next day until there is no memory of him in the stones, or the people who live there. A silent observer, lost and alone. In the house by the sea, the house across the border.

BRUISED

It just appeared one day. A small, but painful bruise. At the back of her upper arm although she couldn't remember banging it. It hurt a bit when her clothes rubbed against it but she gave it no more thought by the time she'd climbed into her beloved, dented, ancient Fiat Panda with its one cracked headlight that made it look like it was winking. As it was Monday she was late, as if every weekend she forgot how to get ready for work. Although she hadn't been sleeping well recently so it was taking her longer to get ready. She caught a twinge now and again through the day but nothing prepared her for when, at home, she undressed to take a shower only to see that the bruise had blossomed.

The next day rain sleeted down which meant she had to spray the engine with WD40 before the car would start. Its many idiosyncrasies only made her love it more. Another dreary day at the office and her arm felt tender whenever she moved it. It must have been one hell of a bump. She phoned her boyfriend to arrange to meet up. Was he going to stay at hers or she at his this time?

She arrived before him, as usual, and settled in with a large glass of Pinot. The pub was the same one they always met in. The same one they'd first met in. Their relationship more like friends with benefits than anything serious, anything leading anywhere. When Richard arrived he didn't apologise for being late. Like always. They hugged and she let out an involuntary sound of pain.

"What's the matter?" Richard asked.

"Nothing, just bashed my arm and got a massive bruise."

He kissed her forehead, she hated that and the fact that just because he was taller than her he thought that he could do this whenever he liked.

"How'd you bang it?"

"Weirdly, I don't remember."

"Were you drunk?" he asked in that sing song way you'd talk to children. Another thing she found annoying about him.

Later, when they were having sex, he grabbed her arm hard and it hurt so much she screamed in pain and couldn't stop crying.

"Perhaps you should get an X-Ray?" he said, after apologising profusely. *Should she?*

The next day, getting dressed, she looked at the massive bruise that took up most of her upper arm and had spread to her elbow. Darkly purple in the centre, fading to ghastly green at the edges. *Perhaps I should get it checked out?* She shook her head, it was only a bruise.

They called Wednesday 'The little weekend' in the office, no planned meetings in the afternoon, the staff making it a tradition to go for a drink after work. Susan, her sometimes friend, sometimes rival, oftentimes drinking partner, saw her wince when moving her arm.

"Something wrong?"

"Not really, just got a big bruise."

"Richard playing rough?" Susan looked sympathetic, but she caught the titillating glint in her friend's eye.

"Nothing like that no."

And like that the whole office knew that she'd hurt herself. It elicited some grunts of sympathy. No big deal.

Later, when she got home and was peeling off her top, she was surprised, and pained, to find that it had stuck to her shoulder where, she saw in the mirror, lacerations leaking clear pus had made her shirt go yellow and crusty and stick to her.

What the hell?

She propped the card for her GP on the side table by her phone. She'd make an appointment in the morning.

When the alarm pulled her from a dark dream, all speed and sound, a mental scream dully echoing into a slow fade, she groped to switch it off and felt a sharp stab in her hand. When she flicked the light on she looked with a stunned horror at her little finger, bent, black, swollen, the nail missing, crusted with blood the colour of the Devil's soul.

She rang the office, begged off sick. She rang Richard, left a message asking him to call her. She rang the GP, tried to make an appointment for that day. When they answered she fake coughed but that triggered a series of real, uncontrollable barking coughs that left her weak, breathless and with a greyness to her vision that was extremely worrying. The apologetic receptionist informed that there were no more appointments today, she'd have to wait till tomorrow, although she did agree that the cough did sound nasty.

With her bowl of muesli balanced on her lap she sat at her desktop and opened Google and scared herself with all the deadly diseases that it could possibly be. Deciding to take a long hot shower she winced when standing up. Her back pulled stiffly. In the bathroom, in the mirror, she looked at another blossoming bruise starting at her shoulder blade and spreading like an ink blot across her back. Now she was scared. She had trouble catching her breath, she touched her side and screamed out in pain and shock as she felt like one of her ribs had become detached. Her diaphragm hurt. She decided to go to the hospital, something was very wrong.

She grabbed her keys from the side table and moved gingerly to her car. Its one winking headlight a mute accusation. The white paint chipped and rusted, looking like old blood, around the cracked light.

She sat carefully and started the car, after the usual cajoling, fiddling with the clutch and prayers to the god of Italian cars. As she moved off there was a definite twinge in her hip and she could hardly move her arm. Unable to turn out of her drive or use the pedals properly she abandoned the car, skewed across the drive, and limped back inside to call a cab. She angrily wiped away her tears with an alien hand, swollen and tender.

What's happening to me?

By the time she got to the hospital she had a high tinnitus and the beginnings of an earache on her right side. She negotiated her way through the emergency room and, amidst her terror, still had time to bewail the fact that doctors were looking younger all the time.

They ran a battery of tests, everything checked out as normal. No broken bones, no dislocations, no fever or problems with heart rate, blood pressure, SATs. They looked at her funnily, as if she was wasting their time, exaggerating. She insisted on blood tests. She'd have to wait for the results.

She was sent home, with some strong painkillers. Advised to keep her appointment with the GP. The young doctor commenting that binge drinking was what doctors call 'very, very bad for you.' She grimaced an ambiguous answer and headed home. She dry swallowed a couple of the torpedo shaped pills and entered a happy place, cocooned in her duvet.

When she woke the next day she was disorientated after another set of nightmares, the sheets ruffled and sweaty, an absence of the usual sounds of traffic, birds, the workmen down the road. When she sat up she realised that she had gone deaf in one ear. One eye puffed up, a constant eeee screeching in the background.

She dragged herself over to the bathroom, her whole right side not seeming to want to obey her. Her head in the mirror was lopsided, her face unrecognisable. She closed her eyes, tears leaked freely. It was not her in the mirror when she opened them, it was the victim. "I'm sorry... I'm sorry." She said between sobs slumping to the floor.

The woman in the mirror looked on, lips compressed, eyes narrowed, brow furrowed.

She gritted her teeth against the pain and crawled back to the bedroom, her hip feeling like it was floating freely, the ball grinding against the outside of the socket; jagged hot pains shot down her leg. Her breath caught; a high, squashed wheeze whistling as each precious breath escaped. Could she make it to the phone? Her right hand was a claw; her arm felt like it belonged to another. She reached left handed for the phone, collapsing as she knocked it to the floor. She was sobbing, the pain was phenomenal; something had become detached in her chest, piercing her over and over again. With each breath the world was going grey.

She stabbed the phone with her finger, its screen wavering in and out of focus.

"Emergency. Which service?"

She managed to mumble "Police."

When the operator came on line she took a deep, painful breath and said "I want to report a hit and run. A couple of weeks ago." The tears still flowed freely but she breathed easier. The woman in the mirror nodded once in satisfaction. "It was me. I did it."

THE INFECTION

I FOUND THESE scraps of paper today. Means I can leave a record, a chronicle of sorts. From my prison, I can see them watching me all the time, with their blank faces and doll-like eyes. They pace up and down outside the window. Their expressions impossible to interpret through the glass, but probably frighteningly blank. I am trapped in these two rooms. In the research centre, two secure rooms, one outer door, one inner door, one large reinforced glass window. There is a bed, a desk, where I found these scraps, and a harsh overhead light I cannot control. The inner room has a drain, water. The outer door is locked tight. No-one is coming in. I am not going out. I am not sure how long it has been, but long enough for everything to go to shit. If you're reading this then you know the score. Let's call this Day 1. It's arbitrary but who cares, it's my memoir.

Day 2 - They are implacable, unforgiving, relentless, omnipresent. It feels good to get words on paper again. However ephemeral they will prove to be. I know what they want from me and it chills me to my very marrow. I will be helpless before them. Like a lamb to the slaughter. If they come in I will fight them, to the best of my ability but I've seen how that's gone for the others. I realise I am doomed. I have food, and drink, and these few scraps of paper but when they grow tired of waiting it will avail me naught. The screams of the others haunt my nightmares. I imagine them coming in, crowding round me, lifting me up, slamming me down, like I've seen them do to the others. I have to stop watching at that point. I don't like to see how it ends. How I'll end.

Day 3 – I had *the dream* again last night. Teeth ripping flesh, blood spurting, hungry dead eyes, high pitched squealing like discordant music. All very disturbing. They watch and they pace and they stare. I am never getting out am I? This is my last will and testament, my legacy and my story. I wish I had longer.

I am trapped, like a rat in a maze, subjected to their malevolent scrutiny. Where are my family? My friends? I think I know how this will end. I am afraid. Stunned with fear, but they say you can get used to anything. However the bright overhead lights hide nothing. I watch and fear. They watch and wait.

My wife and daughter will have to remain anonymous to you gentle reader. I cannot bring myself to visit the past. It is too painful. Suffice to say I am, I was, a family man. I had a job. I did the usual things. I had a mother, father, sisters, colleagues, friends, acquaintances and they have all been taken from me. Ah fuck it, my life is over, everything is over.

What do I want to say here? What do I need to say here? I sleep, I get up, I eat, I stare into space, I watch them watching me, I pace up and down in time with them. I await my death. The infection will rule. I find that this ritual of writing keeps me sane. I will write to the end or until I run out of writing material. Even if I don't wish to explore the past in too much detail here. I hope that you will forgive me.

Day 4 – I sleep when I'm tired, eat when I'm hungry, use the smaller room as little as possible, the smell is becoming too much.

I am stiff this morning, sluggish, cold, I am worried about the food, if there is enough. I am always hungry, not getting enough of something in my diet I guess. Having no access to the outside I cannot see when it is dark or light.

I've no idea if what I am marking as days are actually days. I feel time running down, my clothes becoming looser, life slowly escaping like air from balloon. It is an infection, virus probably, weaponised most likely, like Rabies crossed with Influenza. There needs to be much study. Why do all the bad diseases start with 'flu-like symptoms?'

Day 5 – Not sleeping well, mostly awake, last night. Hands hurt, cramps, writing hard. Spent lots of time banging on window. Shouting. Trying to make them stop. Make them go away. All they do is stare. Exhausted; feel like I've run a marathon. Lack of food? Need more protein. Maybe some vitamin C, I do so hope I'm not coming down with something. I hope the headache is due to dehydration, maybe I'll feel better after a little sleep?

Day 6 – Can't shake bad sound in head, thirsty, eyes sore, hungry, can't focus, words swim, smell much worse. Need food. Feed. Hungry. Meat.

***

ADDENDUM: SUBJECT'S OWN words included in this report are not redacted. Once the infection took hold it progressed fairly rapidly with an overall degeneration in both physical and mental function. As described in the main report and autopsies of the subjects so far, the disease appears to work in three stages. In the first the infected appear normal and fully functioning but are contagious through bodily secretions. The second stage retards function with, as the subject himself puts it, flu-like symptoms. The third stage is the one that holds the most interest to the program. After a quiet period, where bodily functions almost ceased, the subject was vigorous, apparently ravenous and full of rage. Subjects two and three were provided after direct infection through bites from this, our subject zero. It is this author's opinion, in concurrence with the conclusion of the report, that this strain should be studied further to assess if stages one and two can be accelerated. This will then prove to be a very effective weapon against an enemy population.

IT'S ALWAYS THE END FOR SOMEONE

She left Simon another message.

"It's me. He was worse yesterday. I'm going to the hospital now. He'd love to hear from you. I'd love to hear from you. I know, I know, you only switch your phone on once a week when you come down off the mountain top. But… Christ Simon it's coming. The end is coming I… we… Fuck just come home. It's close."

She stabbed the end call button and wiped a tear away. Took several deep breaths, buttoned up her coat and opened the front door. The weather was suitably apocalyptic. The forecast was for winds of fifty mph, with gusts up to eighty. She'd heard someone say on the bus that unusual solar activity was to blame for the weather. She had bigger things to worry about and no time to read the news or watch TV.

She pulled her scarf close and scuttled down the road to the bus stop. She glanced ruefully at the car but had foregone its comforts for her nightly trips. Fucking government; paying hospital parking was a sickness tax.

The bus, when it finally arrived, was steamed up and smelt of wet dog. She sat by the window and wiped a clear area and watched the streets amble past. She remembered when their car had been steamed up, at Bridgend, eating fish and chips, Dad laughing, Mum happy, Simon reading a book about space, and her? She had always tried to hold the family together. Telling jokes, keeping everyone talking to each other. Her eyes misted up yet again. She remembered Dad wiping the steam away and pointing out the stars to them. Simon had got his love of space from him.

Now Mum was gone, Dad was sick and Simon was on the other side of the world staring at the stars through a massive telescope. Actually that bit wasn't even true. The telescope measured radio waves, or X-rays or something and he just studied the computer. Why he couldn't do that online she didn't know. Today was what? Saturday, Simon would be checking his phone tomorrow. Although his tomorrow was several hours behind hers. He hadn't been there when Mum… when it happened. Just blew in for the funeral. She tried to make him stay for a while but no luck. Since Dad had been ill she'd had no time for herself, too busy to find someone to support her, the way she supported everyone else.

Simon's last message, he hadn't called when she was at home, hadn't answered when she phoned back, was about esoterics, the 'cosmic wind' and a breakthrough that'd make him famous. She was glad and angry.

The bus farted to a stop and she glanced out the window to see that it had arrived. Last stop. Final destination. Another tear leaked out of her eye despite her best efforts, she ground her teeth. She swished off the bus to the monumental stone monstrosity that was the hospital; as black as a cancerous lung. Anyone watching would have seen her square her shoulders, like trying to shift a heavy burden, before entering the waiting entrance under sheets and plasterboard still.

They were still working on it, seemed to have been for the longest time, she had no idea what they were doing. The foyer changed weekly, all temporary walls and taped off areas, a constantly changing maze she had to negotiate to the throbbing heart of the hospital. Everyone seemed to take the two massive lifts; the stairs were directly opposite but too much effort for the sick and the well alike.

She climbed aboard a lift alongside a bed; being wheeled from God knows where to places best not thought about. The silent cadaverous old woman in it looking like an injured bird swaddled in clean white sheets and vomit coloured blankets. She averted her gaze from the old dear only to catch one of the porters perving at her. She shuddered and was grateful when they remained in the lift as she got out. The large hall was shaped like a H with narrow corridors like veins heading north and south. She walked down one that went south. To the ward her father was on.

She conscientiously used the alcohol gel and went straight for the third bed on the left. To her father. He was asleep, although nowadays it was hard to tell because he slept with his eyes open. The oxygen mask had slipped and she absent-mindedly straightened it as she kissed his waxy forehead. The tears that had been threatening ganged up and came all together. He had been such a strong man, a tall man, her father; a solid, albeit almost silent presence, throughout her life. Now he was reduced to a few flesh covered sticks and a beak-like face. Where had all his weight gone? It had seemed to boil off him over the last few weeks.

She took her seat, grabbed the book off the bedside table, a Stephen King, his favourite author, and, wiping her eyes, started to read.

She hadn't got far when the nurse came and spoke to her. They had increased his pain meds. They were treating him for an infection. They thought he had pneumonia again.

"Have you managed to get in touch with your brother?" The nurse, whose name she was ashamed to have forgotten, asked.

She shook her head.

"He'll get in touch, on Sunday right?" The nurse said.

She swallowed and blinked away even more tears and nodded. The nurse placed a hand on her arm. "He needs to come soon," she said and there the tears were again. Seriously? She wondered how one person could cry so much. She must have been responsible for dehydrating a lake's worth of water, one plastic cup at a time. The nurse placed one in her hands now and passed her a tissue.

"It won't be long now. He may not even wake." The nurse said sadly, patted her awkwardly on the shoulder and wandered on to the next bed. This held a fat old man, who shat himself every day at around the same time, as the nurses turned him to prevent bed sores. She had not yet become used to the smell.

She smoothed her father's yellow grey hair from his sweaty brow and used a sponge on a stick to wet his lips, as the nurses had shown her. She replaced the mask, sat back down, and started reading again.

Once visiting time was over and she was buttoning up her coat the nurse, who was going off duty, came to see her again.

"Come in early tomorrow love and stay as long as you like. You won't be in the way."

She nodded gratefully. "Thank you."

"Just get that brother of yours to come home, before it's too late."

***

AT HOME SHE sank into an exhausted slumber. She seemed to have no time to herself. She had been visiting him daily for months. Get up, eat breakfast, go to work, nip to the hospital lunchtime, go back to work, go home grab something quick to eat, visiting hours, go home, sleep, repeat.

Today, being Sunday, she slept through till ten am and cursed herself for being such a lazy cow. She got ready and walked out into the wind. It was blowing a gale, a struggle to make headway. At the bus stop she watched as an old woman with a hip problem was blown over. She stood up, ready to go and help when the bus turned up. As it came to a stop she dithered until she saw that two shop assistants from the shop opposite the bus stop had come out to help the old woman. She got on the bus which sailed down the road serene amongst the flying debris: leaves, small branches, litter, all thrown like a giant child was kicking through the streets with glee.

The hospital was unusually empty when she arrived, the bus had been empty too, now she thought about it. She made the usual trip up to the ward. Made sure nothing had changed. She took out the birthday card she'd picked out during a more hopeful time. A picture of Tommy Cooper on the front. A recording of a few of his catchphrases when it was opened. She put it on the bedside cabinet.

"I know it's not your birthday for a few weeks but I thought you'd like to open your card now. It'll cheer you up." Her throat felt swollen, as if she was the one who'd had the surgery. She tucked him in and then glanced at the clock.

She made the long trip outside and tried Simon's number again. It was about nine am in Chile but she didn't care. She needed to get through to him.

"Hello?" A sleepy voice answered.

"Simon? Thank fuck. Why haven't you answered any of my calls?" She was equally angry and relieved. He answered!

"Sis? Wait a second." There was muffled rustling and she thought she heard a woman's voice say, "who is it?" and she definitely heard him say, "it's my sister, I'll be five minutes."

"Sis?" he said, loud and clear.

"Five minutes?" she said coldly.

"Shit. Listen, that was just to mollify Sandra," he said, sounding sheepish.

"Who's Sandra?" she asked.

"No-one special. Listen I have to tell you something important."

"No. You listen Simon. Dad's… He's… Fuck, he's… you need to come home as soon as possible. Shit, it may already be too late. You have to come home. He… it's the end Simon, the end isn't far."

There was silence on the other end.

"Simon?"

She heard him take a deep breath.

"I'm really sorry about Dad but that's just it, Sis. It *is* the end."

"What?" She said, not catching on.

"This is about more than Dad. I don't think I'll be able to come. Like I said I think it's the end," Simon said.

"What do you mean? Why can't you come? Can't you make an effort? For Dad? For me?"

"Look I'm sorry Sis. I really am, I'd love to come but it's just not possible. Remember that thing I said would make me famous? It's coming. There's a massive wind coming and it is going to blow us all away. Everyone." He sounded tired, resigned, wrung out. Pretty much like she felt herself.

"A wind? What? Simon you aren't making sense." She couldn't work out why he couldn't make the trip. "Why can't you just leave it for a few days? Come home?"

"I can't. I can't explain the science behind it quickly but it's coming, today, tomorrow at the latest. It's going to blast away our magnetosphere, it's going to blow on the sun like it's a candle in a draft, there's going to be a solar flare like never before. We're fucked Sis. The planet is fucked. I won't be coming home. Come tomorrow there won't be a home to come to. I'm sorry. I love you. I love Dad too. Let him… let him know for me?"

She could hear him sniff, imagined the tears running down his face.

"So that's it? For everything? I thought… I don't know what I thought, you said it was big, that it'd make you famous?"

"It's much bigger than we thought, we've run the numbers again, sharing it with the world, but the government, ours and others, are burying their heads in the sand. Can't blame them really, what'd it achieve if they told anyone? We think it's going to blast us. At the very least it'll blast the satellites out of orbit, keep the airplanes grounded, fry communications, anything with electricity. Some people may survive it. As long as the cosmic radiation doesn't cook them. I… I'm sorry about everything. Live for yourself tonight. It's our only choice." She heard a woman's voice calling his name in the background.

"Shit…" she said, bewildered.

"Quite. Listen, Sis this is probably the last time we'll speak. Even if the wind doesn't wipe out all life on the planet I'm thousands of miles away and it'll be back to the age of sail, if we're lucky, if we survive this. I'm sorry I've been a shitty brother—"

"Simon—" she tried to interrupt him, he needed to let her speak.

"No let me finish. I should have been there to help you and Dad look after Mum. I'm sorry. I should be there now. I thought I had time. We had time. I… I'm sorry. I love you Sis. Tell Dad… you know. Goodbye Sis-"

"Simon wait!"

The line went dead and she frantically redialled. It went straight to answerphone. "Shit!" she shouted, she redialled and his phone was obviously switched off. "You selfish bastard!" She yelled, then, after a short pause, "I love you too little brother," in a much quieter voice, then texted him and with tears running down her face she walked back to the ward. Could he be right? He seemed pretty sure and the conversation seemed final.

***

WHEN SHE ARRIVED she was surprised that there were people around. Nurses bustled about looking after the patients who sat shell-shocked in their beds in various states of consciousness. Should people know? She thought about shouting it out. People should be with their loved ones. But, she thought sadly, they'd just think she was mad, maybe ask her to leave. Best to leave them alone. Ignorance was bliss. She sat next to her father's bed. Picked up the King novel and started reading.

When her father started to breathe slower, missing breaths, she held his hands and spoke about how Mum loved him, how she loved him, how Simon loved him and, that, as long as there were people alive who knew his name, he would live on and be loved. His eyes stared into the vast unknown. His breath caught, rattled, caught and stopped. A tear fell from her eye onto his cheek, it looked like he was crying. As she kissed his forehead, his muscles were already relaxing, making him look at peace for the first time in months. The lights went out. The sky was filled with an eerie green glow. The northern lights?

At first she thought the silence was just that she could no longer hear her father's breath, but soon realised that all the machines had stopped. All she could hear was the wind, which clawed at the building like a raging demon. She looked at her phone, it was dead. The world held its breath, then people were shouting for the generators to start, rushing around, trying to bring order to chaos. She stood slowly, put the book down, on her father's chest, spine up like a landed moth, then walked to the main hallway, onto the stairs and up. Behind her she heard the shattering of glass, the howling of the wind and many voices raised in a chorus of fear.

***

ON THE ROOF she marvelled at the sight of a dark city which seemed to undulate in the lambent emerald of the light in the sky. Up here the demon wind was ripping the flimsier structures apart and debris flew all about. She fought her way to the edge of the building and hung on to the railing as the wind tried to snatch her away. She wished Simon could have come home, that her mother hadn't had been taken away from her, that her father could hold her and tell her everything was going to be OK. She looked out across the blinded city, hearing the screams carried upon the demon wind. She wished she could see the stars.

THE SOFT SPIRAL OF A COLLAPSING ORBIT

CAITLIN TURNED OFF the klaxons and flashing lights and briefly closed her eyes. The sweeter susurrus of the ship's background life support took moments to re-assert itself. She looked out the view screen at the massive planet creeping ever closer and sighed. There was no one but her to hear the alarms and they had been giving her a headache.

The life support pods stood in mute accusation; hers open like the eye of a judgemental god, the others blank faces, lights off, dark shapes within, corpse heavy. Apart from the last, also open, also empty. She'd done her screaming, her crying; her recriminations were piled high, awaiting the chance to crush her. Now she sat in the relative silence, breathing the stale air with its hint of electrical fire, like the long finish of a distasteful wine.

She stared out of the view screen dully, non-thinking; the great brown ball of roiling clouds compressed her thoughts beneath their weight. *I am going to die.*

She glanced at the instrument panel with its incomprehensible guts on show, all wires and chips like a tangled ball of wool that a cat has played with. The splash of blood led her sliding gaze to the body on the floor. McNeil.

What dark dream had he suffered before the malfunction of his pod that had led to this? She had emerged, groggy, disorientated, into a swirling maelstrom of violence. Her face now puffed and purple from the battering he'd given her, as though it was as much to blame as the instrument panel he'd been taking it out on before she emerged.

Her eyes darted over the screwdriver buried deep into his eye socket. The holes in his thorax and neck like a connect-the-dots picture with a morbid conclusion. She'd been unable to work the other life pods, their alarms lost in the symphony.

The comms, fucked, navigation, fucked, any method of flying this thing, fucked. She was fucked. Life support? A-OK. Nice, caught in the gravity of a giant gas planet and able to live every moment of pulverising pressure as the planet slowly squeezed the vessel in its massive grip.

Many years ago her mother had taken her to a Turner exhibition, or was it Constable? She got those two mixed up. Canvases dipped in murk, lighting storms at play off coastal vistas, sepia tinged frenzied splashes of cloud climbing to black like some angry deity above insignificant figures in the foreground. She envisaged those canvases writ large, on a planetary scale as she looked once again at the roiling brown planet below. Her own personal abyss on a soft spiral of collapsing orbit.

There was no one to hear, no one to see, no one to mourn her passing. She imagined the terse text of the shipping log: Name of ship, dimensions, year & place built, engines, owners, date of wreck, location. Except no one would know the exact location, the homing beacon long silenced. Would anyone even look? Movement made her look down and she saw, with a vague blurred horror, that her hands opened and closed, claw-like, of their own accord. As if they missed the grip of the screwdriver. Could she?

She wondered if she would hear or feel the wind. What the buffeting would feel like? Like every turbulent flight combined and magnified no doubt. Perhaps she'd be smeared on the inside of the cabin long before it was crushed. Her roving, unfocused gaze skipped across the airlock and, like a needle on a vintage vinyl, skipped back again. Could she?

There was nothing to write on, and no final words to write. No bottle to throw upon the sea of stars. Just the long, slow, silent spiral to look forward to. She wished she could talk for one last time to Adam. He'd accused her of robbing him of their future together in their last, bitter argument. But later he'd sent her Scott of the Antarctic's journals, showing he understood; or perhaps it was a message that she was headed for doomed futility. By the time she'd received it, they were deep in training and incommunicado. She'd spent the last weeks before the mission endlessly reinterpreting the gift. Was there some hint of rapprochement? She didn't know, she would never know. She remembered a line from the journal – 'we shall stick it out to the end'. Could she?

IT FALLS

I HAVE NO eyes to see the darkness the bathyal carcass sinks down through. It is given animation only by the bubbles that mark its passage to the abyss. Strange currents, odd phosphorescence, mad creatures: the only witnesses. Stars drift across the sky far away. I instinctively know where one is, a false star, circling, it is my godcommunicator.

The being has given life before, now in its final journey it still has the power to do so. But the life it births this time is different. Unchecked by living systems colonies of bacteria multiply logarithmically. Fungus blooms in lungs the size of cars. Blind exotic shapes.

It was once busy, had volition, intelligence. It only became interesting to the masters once it stopped. Or that is my assumption, for that is when my task started.

My small presence is barely noticeable. The masters await my reports. I will continue to report until it is gone. One data pellet per month. I will stay and sample until no traces remain. Then I will resupply and seek another. I will fulfil my purpose. I send the whispering presence circling above another report.

There was a surface phase. Mobile scavengers part one. Then the gases failed to keep it buoyant. Now it sinks. Still they come and strip the flesh. Tentacled bullets stream past, scouts for larger cousins, eyes more complicated than those that my creators possess. They spurn the necrotising mass. We tumble downwards.

My sensors have counted hundreds of species that have benefitted from its death already. I know there are two more stages to come yet. I have done this before. I will do it again. Message. Acknowledge. Another report.

The first phase draws to a close, the ever thinner soft parts squabbled over by ever smaller scavengers, some armoured, some hunted, some seeking camouflage. The ceaseless web of life. Message. Acknowledge.

The longer, slower, second, enrichment opportunistic stage starts. More armoured beasts. Chitinous polychaetes. I watch them and they never suspect my presence, apart from the ones I sample of course. I track genetic variation across generations; am silent witness of their triumphs and disasters. Every month I report. Message. Acknowledge.

As the months turn into years I work tirelessly. Batteries and engines successfully submit to maintenance enquiries, network remains strong, all is good. I include systems status in my annual reports. They expect it of me.

Picked clean we enter the sulphophilic stage. I watch the Annelids retreat. Their constant movement now absent from the final phase. I am settled. It will be decades yet. I continue to report as the sulphur loving bacteria break down the bone lipids. I still count the number of species in their hundreds. Years pass in the same way. Punctuated via the reports. Until.

Report. Pause. Report. Pause. Not Acknowledge? Protocols consulted. Error detected. Lack of network. I institute a heartbeat ping awaiting an answer and continue to sample. Collate. Build the next report. Two reports. Pause. Not Acknowledge. Three. Many.

Later, mission complete I detach and rise in a turbulence of bubbles. The solar sail deploys. Homing activated. All reports backed up. A fault in the false star, still in the sky but not responding. As I get closer to shore I ping a message to the home base. No Acknowledgement. I perform another systems check.

Perhaps the fault lies with me? But when I see the bodies in the streets I know the fault is not with me.

Some data has already been lost but we are still in the mobile scavenger stage. I sample. I collate. Prepare reports. It is my purpose. There is lots of work to do. Some of their structures will last for very many decades. I keep the heartbeat ping. One day they may recover to a level where they can restart the network. I collect data against that hope.

One for sorrow,

Two for luck; (or mirth)

Three for a wedding,

Four for death; (or birth)

Five for silver,

Six for gold;

Seven for a secret,

Never to be told;

Eight for heaven,

Nine for hell

And ten for the Devil's own self

FIVE FOR SILVER

'Dreamy', 'Daydreamer', 'Away with the fairies', 'Head in the clouds' That's what all my school reports said. You'd think they were millstones wouldn't you? Positively negative traits not desired by any employer? Well Mrs Facet was different. She looks for children like me. Came and sought me out especially. Mrs Facet, with Albert, Alfred and Algernon. Came to my school. Stood in front with the teachers at assembly, like a heron and three crows, and pointed to me.

"That one," Mrs Facet said. I heard her perfectly, with her finger at the end of a tweed-sheathed arm pointing unerringly at me. "Are you sure?" Mr Garner, the Headmaster said, his head particularly glistening and shiny. No surprise we all called him Slap. "Mmmm? Yes of course. I am not used to being questioned. Make him ready for four pm." At this Mrs Facet took out a large pocket watch, on a long silver chain, just like you see on the old films or the new films about old times. She took one more sweeping glance around the room, tutted, clicked her fingers at the Al's (although I didn't know to call them that yet) and trooped out. Her heels clacked, their shoes squeaked, loud in the silence echoing in the large hall but I could see lots of the other kids looking at me. It wouldn't be long before the whispering started.

At four pm precisely I stood outside the main gate, having

been manhandled there by Mr Humphries, (Hump the Grump) the Games master. By means of pushing, pulling, grunting and growling he'd got me where he wanted me. "Stay!" he shouted, his bushy eyebrows marching towards his hairline, and, as if thinking better of it, possibly because they'd get lost in the thick forest of hair, they shuffled back to above his eyes. He scratched his shaggy beard, glanced at his watch and lifted the whistle he wore round his neck to his lips, a nervous habit we all emulated in the silliest way possible when he wasn't looking. He grunted and turned around, almost falling over me. "Stay!" he barked a second time before wandering off back towards the playing fields, seemingly job done.

I sighed theatrically and looked from one end of the school building to the other. When I turned my eyes back to the driveway I was surprised to see a small car, a battered Fiat Panda, sat waiting for me, like a dejected puppy that is sure a walk is out of the question. Inside were Mrs Facet, in the driver's seat, with a strange hat upon her head and leather driving gloves and the Al's sat in the back sometimes shifting en masse one side to another as Al in the middle (I forget which one, they're so interchangeable) elbowed one or other brother to try and get more room. Mrs Facet opened the passenger door and gestured me inside.

As soon as I sat down, and closed the door, the car leapt away. Mrs Facet stared ahead. "Seatbelt!" she barked. I struggled with the seatbelt as we were taking the long slow bend, neither slowly nor indeed long, Mrs Facet interrogated me.

"Name?"

"Bentley, miss."

"Like the car?"

"Yes, miss."

"Age?"

"Thirteen."

"How many dreams do you have per night, Bently?"

"It's with an 'e,' miss."

"Oh yes of course, well, Bentley?"

"Erm I don't know."

The car came skidding to a halt as the seatbelt clicked into place and although I was thrown forward the belt did its job admirably and I didn't go straight through the windscreen.

"Gate!"

I belatedly realised it meant I had to get out and open the gate. When I got back in the door had hardly closed when the car leapt off again.

"Don't know?"

"You don't know what, miss?"

"You don't know."

"You don't know what I don't know?" I said confused.

"You don't know the number of dreams you have at night?"

"Oh that. Erm five, miss?"

I don't know why I said five. It happened to be both the right number and the answer she was looking for though. One of the Al's said, "five for silver," and when I turned around to look they all grinned at me, eerily, similar grins on their triplet faces, all with the same lank black hair and neat black suits. They may have been older than me, but if so, not by much.

"Miss? I know you don't like questions, miss, but no-one has told me what this is about and I would appreciate it if you told me, miss." I got to the end of this little speech and Mrs Facet took a long look at me, which was alarming as the traffic flowed by on either side of us.

"Yes. Well. You, my boy, have been chosen to assist me in a great matter. I am, and I say this with no false pride, the best Biblionaut in the country, Ah." She said raising a hand, index finger held aloft to forestall my obvious question. "And I have a grave, an onerous, an oath bound duty to perform. For which I require the services of a Dreamer." There was a faint coughing from the back of the car. "And the able assistance of the etc. etc." The car swerved around a corner and came to a dead stop. "We're here."

'Here' seemed to be a plain corner shop with an olive green

exterior, shuttered and with a faded awning. '*Facet & Co.*' neatly painted over the door. '*Books for the discerning customer*' on the door itself. I climbed out after Mrs Facet who tossed her gloves and hat through the open door as the three Al's clambered out, looking a little disapprovingly at me. "Etcetera, etcetera," I heard one of them mumble. I'm not sure which of them. Probably the one who claimed to be the oldest at that point.

"*Facet and Co*" Mrs Facet said, first pointing to the shop then to herself and finally to the three Al's. "Shall we?" One of the Al's raised the shutter and we all walked inside. The inside of the shop was redolent of aged paper as row upon row of leather bound tomes lined all the available walls, spilled over onto all the available surfaces and dripped onto the floor, forming book stalagmites. A rather large, fat, orange tom cat eyeballed me briefly and licked its lips, before slumping back into slumber. We trooped through the outer shop, before going through a moth-eaten velvet curtain and into a tiny kitchenette where one of the Als lit the stove, another filled a kettle and the third washed up four cups. Mrs Facet lifted a bone china teacup and saucer, with blue and red flowers upon it, which matched the tea pot. Alfred picked up a 'World's best xxxxxx Alfred' mug, I couldn't tell what the hidden word was below the permanent marker but Alfred had been scrawled on underneath in a childish hand. Albert held a mug saying 'This is a round Tuit. We said that one day we'd get one of these.' On the bottom, a little sticker saying Albert, one corner unstuck so it looked like it said Alber. Algernon picked up a plain white mug. Mrs Facet took in my lost expression, my school uniform and the satchel clasped to my chest and asked "Tea?" I nodded. Which caused the three Al's to go on a voyage of discovery for a fifth cup. Eventually finding one that looked like a freebie from a chocolate company, that they'd been using to keep the cat's cream in in the fridge, which they poured out into a saucer and had no sooner put it on the floor than the cat appeared, purring and lapping it up.

"So. Our mission. You sleep. We travel into your dreams.

Specifically the ones about the ocean. There's a good chap. Do the job and get out."

"I'm sorry. What?"

"Dreams. Ocean. Job. End of."

I looked to the three Al's. They looked back. Blanks.

"Can you just go over that bit again?"

Mrs Facet held up a finger whilst the kettle came to the boil. One of the Al's filled the kettle. Another took out a pocket watch, the third picked the kettle up like a crystal ball and swilled it about counter clockwise. Meanwhile the first returned with a spoon and at a nod from the one with the watch struck it sharply which prompted the third to place it gently upon the table. Mrs Facet poured tea into her own cup, and mine. The three Al's poured for themselves, one after the other.

"Which bit?"

"Erm the bit where you explained what's going to happen."

"So all of it then?"

"Well, er, yes."

"Let me use an analogy. Your brain is the car, your dream of the ocean is the fuel and we are going to drive to our destination using the fuelled up car."

"Nope, that's not any clearer."

"Fine."

Silence. I couldn't stand it.

"Fine?"

"Fine!"

"Oh, er, okay then."

"Show him where to sleep."

Algernon, I know it was him as he put down the plain white mug, gave me a rather sad smile and gestured for me to follow him. "Bentley," I said as we walked up the narrow stairs, which was covered with yellow wallpaper. "I know," he whispered walking slowly up in front of me, his hand rubbing against the wallpaper, which I noticed was shiny at around hand height. "No, I mean, my name's Bentley, what's yours?" He turned his head and his sad eyes looked at me for a second. "Algernon. My brothers are Alfred, he's the oldest currently, and Albert."

"Pleased to meet you."

"Likewise. This is you." We arrived at the top of the stairs and directly opposite a door. Painted a muddy blue colour. The door was ajar, inside, a small room painted to resemble the ocean. Waves crashed at head height, seagulls argued on the ceiling. Below the water porpoises frolicked and the floor was painted yellow, like sand, with crabs and shells. The bed resembled a giant clam.

"It's er. Well I'd say nice but... look I don't want to be rude but... it's a bit weird isn't it?"

"Weird." He looked at me in that expressionless way the Al's have, that I was beginning to find a little creepy.

"Yes all the sea stuff."

"That's for the job."

"Yes about that. I'm not clear on what's going on."

"You go to sleep."

"And."

"And nothing. That's your job. You go to sleep."

"Oh, er, OK, what was all that stuff about dreams being petrol and my brain being a car?"

"Don't worry about it."

"Erm. OK"

"Off you go."

"What?"

His held the door open whilst trying to direct me inside, like a traffic policeman directing cars to pass.

"All you want me to do is go to sleep?"

"That's right."

I walked over the threshold and over to the bed with its seaweed coloured sheets.

"Salt dreams," Algernon said closing the door.

I sat on the bed and looked around. I got up and peered under the bed, walked around the room, went back and sat on the bed. Well this was most odd. It appeared that I had been brought out of school to a strange house to go to sleep. I could hear mumbling downstairs before music started up. I'm not sure what sea shanties are, but I strongly suspected they were playing them downstairs.

Now Mr Garner and Mr Humphries both seemed in on this. And they wouldn't wish me harm. There'd be hell to pay with my parents for a start. I looked at the provided pyjamas. Black silky leggings and a black and white striped top. OK, best way to find out what was going on was to play along. I got changed and got into bed. Under the pillow I found several books including *20,000 leagues under the Sea* and *Moby Dick*. I flicked through *Moby Dick* for a bit but the words were quite difficult so I put it back where I found it and lay down. I expected I'd have a problem going to sleep but head, pillow, light. Maybe there was something in the tea; I wondered why it tasted like oranges.

***

THE SEAGULLS' CRIES sound like drunken sailors laughing, the sun whips my back and the salt sting of the ocean is in my eyes. The boat pitches and yaws, its timbers creaking amiably. The sailors hum a sea shanty, or a close approximation of such, or what I assumed to be such. The captain stands in front of me. "Mr Bently?"

"With an e sir."

"Ah yes of course. Mr Bentley what do you think you're doing?"

"Erm well. I think I'm swabbing the deck sir."

"Swabbing is it?"

"Yes. Although I'm not sure what swabbing involves."

"I can see that. It's the brig for you Bentley." He stops roaring for a moment and leans in close. "You do know what a brig is don't you?"

"I think so."

He stands back at his full height and recommences roaring.

"Good. Then it's the brig for you. Along with the other troublemakers."

Two pirates appear, one on either side of me, and carry me over to a hole in the deck which they throw me down.

It's gloomy, and cooler in the brig, which I imagine poorly to be honest. But well enough for there to be a bit of table in it. Around which are Mrs Facet and the Al's. "Yes. Well didn't I tell you he had a rare gift gentlemen?" Mrs Facet arched an eyebrow as I land close by. "Well done Bentley. Now make sure to stay asleep so we can get this job done." Mrs Facet takes out her massive pocket watch and checks the time before she turns it over and presses a button and another part pops open. It's a hidden compass. "Gosh. That's rather clever," I say. Facet glances up but dismisses my outburst.

"Got him." She pulls out a proper old fashioned cloth-like parchment and unfurls it. On it is a map like none I've ever seen before. It is a patchwork of book covers in a myriad of shapes, colours and sizes with fonts of all types. "Cor!" I say. She takes out what looks like a protractor and makes a few measurements on the map and pens marks in a small blue notebook she has open on her lap. She reels off a string of numbers and letters that make no sense to me but the three Al's start drawing a chalk outline against the hull. It's a crude chalk door. When they open it I am taken aback. As not only does it open, onto a tropical island no less, but the sea doesn't come rushing in. "Gentlemen," Mrs Facet says. Albert does an 'after you motion' to Alfred who mimics his brother and gestures for Algernon to go through first. Algernon turns and looks at me. "How about Bentley goes first?" He says and before I know it they are ushering me through the door.

As I go through, I drop about a foot, which I'm not expecting, so I'm picking myself up off the dust-like soft white sand when a pirate, who I hadn't spotted until this moment, points his sword at me. His stick-like arms poke out of ratty clothes that have seen better days. His sword looks the business. I clamber up and see, over the pirate's shoulder, a hole in the air, the other side of which has Facet & Co jumping through as quietly as they can. Mrs Facet pulls out a large gun and points it at the pirate, Albert struggles under the weight of a large Gladstone bag and Algernon, the last through, pulls the door closed behind him and the air appears to be continuous. No trace of a hole ever existing.

"Put the sword down please, Mr Silver."

Silver looks from me to the Al's and Facet and lets the sword drop to the sand where it bites and stands for a breath or two before toppling and flicking sand up. Silver puts his hands on his hips and says, "Well this is a pickle to be sure." He hops from one bare foot to the other. That sand must be hot. "What'll it be boys. Be we friends or be we enemies?"

Facet sighs, consults her pocket watch that Silver nakedly covets, and sighs again.

"Mr Silver, in approximately ten years you have to appear in a bestselling novel. And you have to have one leg." Silver, who is staring at the watch, looks up sharply "What?"

I echo him "What?" I am ignored by all parties. I decide to wait and see what happens. After all this is my dream.

"I'm afraid Mr Silver that we are here to take your leg."

"Wait, can you go over that bit again."

"Which bit?"

"Something novel, something leg."

"So all of it?"

"Yes."

"In ten of your years you will be a major character in a book called Treasure Island in which you'll menace a small boy whilst hopping around on crutches on account of you only having one leg. Clearly you currently have two legs. We are here for one of them."

"You want me leg?" The poor man seems bewildered. I sympathise.

"Grab him."

Silver turns and makes a run for it. Facet shoots into the air. "Stop or I'll shoot you. In the leg." Deciding that's a risk he's willing to take, or perhaps he just hadn't heard, Silver keeps running and appears to be well practised at it. Facet stands edge on to him, draws a bead, closes one eye and cocks her head so she's looking down the barrel, and takes a second shot. Which misses. "Damn." She takes a large breath, holds it and slowly exhales squeezing the trigger. The gun bucks, there is a puff of smoke and in the distance, Silver stumbles and falls. "Bring the bag," Facet says and we troop down the beach to where Silver lies clutching his leg.

"Nasty wound you have there. Luckily I have my medical equipment. Boys, it looks like we must perform an amputation."

"No. Please. Not the leg. Not the leg!" Silver attempts to fight them, and as they wrestle I say, "This can't be right." Alfred appears to be dextrous with a syringe and soon has Silver unconscious. "Hey!" I shout as Mrs Facet says, "prepare him."

"Yes?"

The Al's are cutting away one leg of the trousers and painting the leg with something red. Iodine?

"What are you doing? You can't just cut someone's leg off!"

"You've read Treasure Island?"

"Yes."

"He's Long John Silver."

"What? How?"

"He must have one leg in ten years' time when Stevenson imagines him for the first time."

"What? How? No I was right the first time. What?"

"Look, I don't have any time to explain."

"OK now I'm going to wake up," I say, "one, two… "

"Wait!"

"Explain."

"Okay I'll explain. No it'll take too long, I'll summarise. Biblionauts." Here she points at herself and the poised Al's who all appear to be wearing butcher aprons and are looking at me in that blank way they have. "Yes," I say, I'm not quite sure what a Biblionaut is but assume it's something to do with travelling in books. "The world of dreams, myths, legends and ideas," she says doing a sweeping motion all around taking in the beach, and the sea beyond as well as the whole island. "Dreamer," she says pointing to me. "Door," she says still pointing at me. "Writers get their ideas from the place of myths and legends. Here. It is non-contiguous and atemporal." I frown. "It is in many places and many times," she says. I make an 'ah!' noise.

"It's leaky you see. Now, every time a book has to be reprinted it is written again. This is a big secret. Borges nearly gave it away but a colleague spotted it in time and fixed it. "Sometimes," she continues "there are disturbances in the doobrie. Things are copied down incorrectly, or one of the copyists gets ideas above their station and makes changes."

I'm confused again

"Just go with it," she whispers. "And those disturbances can lead to a story going, well wrong. The inspiration juice ceases to flow and a book can die if the author doesn't get the right inspiration at the right time. Biblionauts spot this and take action. Like now." She nods at Silver.

"Wait, an author gets inspiration from this place?"

"Yes."

"Then writes a book. That makes changes in this place."

"Yes."

"Then someone copies that book wrong."

"Yes."

"That poisons the inspiration that allowed the book to be written in the first place."

"You've got it."

"That makes no sense whatsoever."

"Whoever said dreams and stories have to make sense. Although they do have an underlying truth."

"I don't understand."

"This has to happen. Now be a good fellow and go down

the beach a ways and keep a look out."

I walk off. Well, I don't think I could stop them. I am thinking furiously though. It makes a certain kind of dream logic I suppose. When they're finished they walk up to me. They have cleaned themselves off.

"OK Bentley. Ready for another dream?"

"Another?"

"You've four more in you remember. Now what do you know about Captain Ahab?"

THE CASE OF THE MURDERS IN THE RUE MORGUE

THE NAME'S BENTLEY, with an e, and I'm a Biblionaut. Well strictly speaking I'm the Dreamer in the team of Biblionauts run by Mrs Facet, the others in the team being the three Al's. If Mrs Facet in her tweed suit was a heron, and the three Al's in their monkey suits were crows then that left me, in my grey uniform, the pigeon. And I've never trusted pigeons. Our job, to fix anomalies in the Place of Myths and Legends, where writers get their ideas.

After the case of Long John Silver's second leg we were on R&R when Facet announced she'd bought a limousine. State of the art, Dreamcraft 2.0 powered by REM (Rotating Electro-Magnets). I didn't understand the technology but it meant they could drive into the dream portals I created in my sleep and so reach further than ever before, because we no longer had to walk anywhere.

"We've got a case," Alfred, currently the youngest of the three Al's said.

"Tell me." Mrs Facet ordered. We gathered round.

"Paris, Le Rue Morgue, a peculiar and uncanny crime solved by a certain Mr Sherlock Holmes, on his holiday apparently." Alfred supplied.

"Why's that a case?" I asked as the others looked at each other with worried expressions. Mrs Facet turned her stare on me and I felt like a Beatle being examined by an entomologist.

"We really do need to catch you up on your education Bentley."

"Yes, miss."

"The Rue Morgue murders should have been solved by C. Auguste Dupin. Poe, not Doyle."

I nodded as though I understood, seeing in the background Albert looking a bit uncomfortable, I guess he hadn't known the details either.

"Paris or London?" Alfred asked.

Facet looked at me, "London, it'll be easier for our dreamer. Let's go and have a word with the great detective."

We spent the rest of the day preparing the room, setting up the usual paraphernalia that would allow me to dream of the correct place, and time. I fell asleep to the sound of Bow Bells.

The limousine cruised down Baker street and Mrs Facet brought it to a stop outside number 221b. Holmes was exactly how I expected him. It seemed that he'd been on holiday in Paris when the news of the murders broke, the fact that numerous witnesses had heard a man speak, but couldn't agree on what language was spoken had peaked his interest, and he had decided to investigate.

Mrs Facet asked many questions and seemed to get more and more flustered. Eventually when she asked how Mr Holmes had travelled to Paris things became clearer, and at the same time murkier.

"I took the train," said he.

There was a long pause where we all looked at one another.

"All the way there?" Mrs Facet asked innocently.

"Of course." The detective looked as though something had just occurred to him. Very quickly, in case he started to investigate us, Facet got us out of there.

"To the train station?" Alfred asked when we were all seated,

Facet had her hands on the steering wheel, but made no attempt to start the car. Albert squirmed on the back seat and I saw that Mrs Facet had noticed, her eyes narrowed.

"To Paris, before the start of case investigating the murders. We must put things back on track. Then we'll investigate the anomaly."

In Paris I was given the task of delivering the news direct to Dupin whilst the others made sure that Holmes didn't hear it, a much more difficult task I think.

I delivered the news of EXTRAORDINARY MURDERS to Monsieur Dupin and his companion to which Dupin seemed singularly interested. He and his companion were deep in conversation when I left. I dare say that if they had not had the papers delivered at that exact point they would never have got involved. Which raised a question in me. How come it was necessary for me to deliver the papers, if the story could not progress without them. I consulted the copy of the story Facet had given me. It mentions that the main character and his assistant were strolling down a dirty street then: 'Not long after this, we were looking over an evening edition of the *Gazette des Tribuneaux* ... ' It seemed that Poe had glossed over my role in his story.

I met the others at Gar du Nord and caught up with their activities, which mostly involved paying off news buskers and preventing the papers from reaching Holmes's hotel. All three editions. It appeared we'd put things to rights and the first detective was again Monsieur Dupin, although Holmes would always be the greatest in my opinion.

"All that's left is to work out why there is a train direct from London to Paris, in the 1880's." Mrs Facet mused aloud.

"Erm," Alfred started, going a rich shade of puce.

Mrs Facet narrowed her eyes.

"Well you see ... " Albert started "I didn't think any harm would come of it."

"No harm would come of *what?*" Facet asked icily.

"Of, er, well … taking the limousine for a spin."

"When was this?" Facet demanded.

"A couple of nights ago. When you were at the library. I only wanted to meet Wells's Time Traveller and ask him some questions. He was awfully interested in the car, and the REM, I er, may have told him how it works. He said he'd love to discuss it with his good friend Brunel."

Mrs Facet pinched the bridge of her nose, "how could *you*, of all people, have been so stupid?"

"I'm sorry. Brunel's not in the story. I didn't think --"

"No you didn't." Facet interrupted. "As usual it's up to us to make things right. Boys, we're going to Richmond."

One for sorrow,
Two for luck; (or mirth)
Three for a wedding,
Four for death; (or birth)
Five for silver,
Six for gold;
Seven for a secret,
Never to be told;
Eight for heaven,
Nine for hell
And ten for the Devil's own self

THE AMNESIA-RIDDEN HILLS

WHAT IS LEFT behind? Open spaces are colonised by successive generations of green invaders until delineation of man-made and natural becomes impossibly irrelevant. Built environments become unbuilt as time and nature unpick brick from brick, divorcing form and structure. Annexation by bird and beast, moss and flower reverses any intentionality, any imposition by man on the land.

***

I AM FLYING across the sea to the island. Wind is one of my enemies, yet I have, for now, broken it like an unruly and giddy horse being ridden for the first time. My seat offers some solace of solidity even though the whole bubble of spun metal bucks and kicks turbulently. I glance at fellow passengers, charcoal grey clad forms, splashes of colour around their throats the only frippery they allow themselves. They do not interest me.

I read again the email that lays crumbs for the wild geese I must entice within my grasp. Certain words and phrases are highlighted in urine yellow; 'thousands of years old,' 'previously unknown to science,' 'fundamental,' 'unprecedented.' Enough meaning beneath the hyperbole to winkle me out from behind my impatient desk.

I glimpse the clock. I will land a very short time after I took off, is that objectively or subjectively? I am indifferent to the difference. Going against the flow. Time is another enemy of mine, the greatest perhaps, one against which any small victory needs to be celebrated. I shut down my laptop and close my eyes. I've some moments of calm before the obligation of seatback upright, seatbelt fastened, compliance.

I follow the barking crowds of besuited businessmen, ambling ever further behind them. Stale air wafts exhaustedly along the shabbily carpeted corridors. Listless refugees are untidily scattered across seats that are not designed for comfort. Grim clouds chase each other across the sky like battleships at war. If it is a wasted journey at least I will have seen the island, I recall sarcastically.

I corral the various sand coloured bags onto the trolley with its inevitable rebellious wheels that have been conceived by spiteful, resentful designers. I wave the pocket full of permissions, represented in coloured stamps in the cardboard square of my passport, at a bored official and manoeuvre my parsimonious packages into the arrivals hall. A full concourse empty of any liaison, any procurer of conveyances, any agent of onward travel. An observer may describe my sigh as being one of exasperation and displeasure but it is a much greyer emotion than that.

My mobile phone beeps. My arrival at this blighted island is only of interest to the network provider it seems. I decide to save the joy of refreshing my inbox until the car journey. I'm all about the self-restraint. I head to the taxi rank. I join the shuffling queue. Taxis slink into place, gobble up young lovers, families, cabals of businessmen and lonesome singletons before leaping into the traffic with their prizes greedily secreted away.

After some desultory pointing at print-outs and refusal on both sides to try each other's languages, I am enticed into a faded interior redolent of synthetic pine. We slalom into town. Taxi journeys the world over are the same. Taxi drivers are the same no matter the language. There is a certain Zen to such journeys. I have ceased paying attention. Emails loaded keep my eyes and hands busy and even occasionally engage the brain. At the hotel there is a similar point and mime to get the key. Hotel rooms may show more variety but it is neither exciting nor necessary to mention it in polite company.

Phone.

Unlock.

Scroll.

Green button.

"What time did you land?"

"The time it said on the email I sent you. The one you replied to."

"Ah okay, so you are at the hotel now?"

"Yes."

"Which one?"

"The one in the email I sent you."

"The one I replied to? Got you. I'll be there in, oh, thirty minutes give or take. This is all very exciting isn't it?"

I agreed that, yes, excitement was a valid emotion to feel at this point, made the necessary small arrangement of location and time alignments and ended the call. I closed my eyes. Calm.

✳✳✳

JEREMY WAS ONE of the interchangeable interns that our industry is afflicted by. Eager, solicitous, to a fashion, and just a little bit incompetent. No, that is unfair of me. It is less of an incompetence, more a lack of experience, a naivety. Amounts to the same thing though. Things I shouldn't need to do myself, I need to do myself. At least there is a minimum of fuss to get into the transport. The driver knows his job. We are sped down city roads, swished through country gates, sloshed over fords and bumped over fields. It is early, cold, interminably grey, in short it is usual for this island.

"We have to walk from here."

"Far?" I have resorted to one word sentences already.

"Mile or so. It's very boggy though; hope you don't mind getting your feet dirty!"

Jeremy bounds ahead, eager to show the way, bouncing around like an excitable puppy. Youth.

At least the walk warms me; although I reflect that once we stop, the layer of sweat my body is profligately producing will freeze in the glum air. Water, a greater enemy than wind, a swifter enemy than time, the universal solvent. I glug at the metal flask, cold against my lips, making my teeth throb, my throat shiver, my insides cringe. I glance at the sky; somewhere up there is the same sun that blisters my skin at home. The grey seems un-natural, the result of some man-made disaster, an environmental catastrophe. How do the locals stand it being so grey? All the time? A brace of black and white birds fly overhead calling to each other in their alien language. Birds, beasts of all kinds, are enemies too. At least sunshine, that great enemy, has been defeated here.

It is a climb, then a slippery slide into the maw of the cave, its blind attendant mouth forever waiting for prey. We abandon some of the bags at the mouth immediately. We'll need to recover them later I suppose. Jeremy grins and says, "tents" like that explains all the mysteries of the universe. I shrug. The guides give us helmets and we look at each other and I reflect that we look like miners from another cold grey land out of time. Jeremy smirks. I doubt much passes through his head at this moment at all. He takes a photo of me with his phone, then a self-portrait. I try not to grimace. I briefly wonder what he'll say about me to his 'friends' on the social medias. I decide I don't care.

Overalls on.

Helmets on.

Lights on.

We descend. Jeremy keeps up a constant inane commentary. His voice fades in and out of my consciousness whilst I listen to the echoes. Occasionally I shush him and pretend to listen. "For bats," I tell him. I abhor bats. There are no bats. There is blissful silence when I shush him though. The sounds of our breathing, slip sounding stones and an occasional drip that disappears as we journey inward, breath is a lesser enemy and here it is seen.

After some spelunking favourites; tight passages, wet crawls, drops with unknown depths, we enter what Jeremy says is a dry water course. A river ran through here. Long ago. This is as far as one of the guides will go apparently. This information seems to be a surprise to everyone, including him. I wander off whilst they argue. Away from their voices, take a corner, another, I feel alone. I close my eyes. Calm. Flapping. Bats, birds? Several pairs of feral eyes glow in the darkness but disappear as I turn my head to see. Jeremy's hand on my shoulder makes me jump. I didn't hear him. It has eventually been agreed that the guide will go back and set up camp. Jeremy grins. "Time to go on, Professor," he says. His eyes do not glow.

A little further on Jeremy shows me the signs that the first explorers of the cave saw. The holes. The smooth places. The discoloured and chipped places. It takes a great deal of imagination to see the missing: jetties, sleeping areas, campfires. These things were guessed at. At first that is. I hear the fluttering of wings again. My torchlight picks out glistening rocks, but no birds. It's much more likely to be bats. We are too far in for birds.

At our next stop we talk about the weather. These islanders, it seems to be all they can talk about. They do get more of it than I am used to though. It should apparently be sunny when we return to the surface. One enemy denied passage here. As we make ready to set off I hear the wings again. I ask for silence. Jeremy looks annoyed. The two guides glance at each other. None of them hear anything. "Come on professor, there is more habitation through here and in an hour or two we'll see the gold."

Ah yes, that metal, immune to most of my enemies, incorruptible gold. The ornamentation people choose to bedeck themselves in. Like the ridiculous stud Jeremy wears. Gold can only tell you so much. It is the ephemeral stuff that is more important. The possibility that pictures, habitations, household items are preserved here. Dodging my various enemies. That's what has drawn me, not gold. I let Jeremy think whatever he wants though.

As we enter the large chamber, it shows signs of recent exploration, colourful ropes left behind like prayer strings nailed to the rock. I again hear the fluttering of wings and, as I glance wildly around, eyes glow phosphorescently from the darkness. Six pairs. I turn and get Jeremy's attention as he sets up the abseil. "Look!" I command and turn back. There are no eyes. The cave is silent. He is polite "What do you see Professor?"

"I thought … nothing, never mind." As he goes back to sorting out the ropes I shrug. I close my eyes. Calm. Calm. "Ready?" Jeremy asks holding out the ropes. We abseil down without incident. "This is the first of the towns," he explains. Town seems a misnomer at first but it does seem as though the people who once lived here, an uncountable time ago, had carved a number of habitations from the cold unforgiving rock that could be said to be enough for a town full of folk. I suspend judgement. I had visited the cave dwellings of Cappadocia as preparation for this but this island, this cave, this space feels different. There is a sudden breeze and I intuit a gliding shape has swiftly passed by. "Have you heard any animals in this cave?" I ask Jeremy. He grins. "We are the first living beings to see this cave since it was blocked thousands of years ago. Well apart from maybe some dumb insects." Insects are an enemy too of course. I try to shake off that feeling. Should I tell him about the eyes? "Come on, Professor, I want to show you their dwellings." I shake my head.

It is obvious after the first habitation that this is indeed the find of the century, and deserving of all the highlighted words and phrases that had attracted me. The first habitation, by itself, would take many hours of study. I longed for some proper instruments. My mind was busy cataloguing, and turning over the possibilities: tenure, grants, it would be career defining. I was unprepared, when I looked up to see where Jeremy and the guides were, to see a black and white bird sat on the windowsill of the rude dwelling. It peered at me, perhaps trying to work out what sort of specimen I was. I stood - the sudden movement made it fly off. "Jeremy!" I shouted. He came immediately. "Did you see the bird?" I ask. He hasn't. He now looks curiously at me. Birds, this deep? It's unknown. We pass it back and forth for a bit. He is sure it may have been a bat or a large moth that I saw from the corner of my eye. I doubt even myself. "Ok, let's go see the gold, all this will still be here," Jeremy says. There is now a hint of condescension in his voice.

We climb up a set of roughly hewn steps and enter a much larger dwelling. Perhaps a gathering house. There are a set of half a dozen seats in a rough semi-circle scattered around three of the edges of the roughly hewn cavern and on each of them a simple golden bracelet of twisted thread-like metal. What could be the purpose of this? There is a shout outside and Jeremy and I look at each other. "Stay here, I'll go check what they want." He leaves. I go over to the first seat and take a closer look at the bracelet. As I do I hear Jeremy shout, the three men outside appear to be excited. I hurry to the door and look out, their torchlight is some way away, Jeremy's moving towards them. I turn around, the better to climb down backwards, when the room in front of me is suddenly filled with feathers as birds explode from somewhere. I see a half dozen black and white shapes before my foot misses the step and I topple backwards. I am too shocked to cry out. I fall through the blackness. I did not think that the ground itself would be my worst, and final, enemy.

One for sorrow,
Two for luck; (or mirth)
Three for a wedding,
Four for death; (or birth)
Five for silver,
Six for gold;
Seven for a secret,
Never to be told;
Eight for heaven,
Nine for hell
And ten for the Devil's own self

WAYMARKER

"So what do you think Prof?"

"Well, Detective, it's a bit elaborate I suppose. It comes from the same place as putting one rock on top of another, in the wilderness, when you want to leave a waymarker."

"So you think it's a waymarker?"

"Possibly, possibly."

"Do you think there's any significance in the species?"

"Probably not, just size, guess our killer couldn't find a hummingbird to top it off."

"I hope you're not going to chew the end of that pencil, those birds could be covered with anything."

"Good point."

"So based on this tableaux what is the killer telling us?"

"This death. That poor woman there. It's merely a marker upon the dark path our killer is taking."

"You expect to find more victims?"

"Yes. The staging is quite elaborate. He's left feathers from seven birds, the quills jammed beneath the nails. It is likely he did that before she died. We'll know better on the autopsy I guess. Not sure if that means she's the seventh victim or the number seven is important to him. I'd put money on the latter, at least I hope it doesn't mean that there will be six victims we've not found yet."

"But you do expect more?"

"Yes. He's killed before. He's developed a style."

"Hey you two, have you seen this?"

"What have you got there Constable?"

"It's a blog. Looks like they've given our killer a nickname already."

"How did they know so soon? Get me the details on who runs that blog, and all the visitors."

"What's the nickname?"

"The Seventh Magpie."

THE CAT'S GOT IT

It was the cat. I was sure of it. It had never liked me. It must have been planning this for a while. The bastard. It was getting me back for that time I went away for the weekend and forgot to feed it. Damn the landlord and his stupid cat. Black as a pervert's soul it was with emerald spiteful eyes. I'd never liked it.

Whilst I cooked, whilst I ironed, whilst I read a book. Every time I glanced up it'd be there, staring in, watching me on its cat TV, occasionally shuffling round the garden into new positions but always careful to never get too close to another's territory, playing cat chess. Every so often I'd have to go throw water over a pair of them fighting or having sex, usually I couldn't tell the difference.

It was definitely the cat. No other explanation fit. It wasn't my girlfriend. She liked the cats of course, secretly fed them too I bet, enticed them into the garden with meat or fish. She wouldn't have known where I kept it. Wouldn't have deigned to touch it either if I knew her. Good job too, wouldn't want too many questions. It wouldn't be 'is this ham?' this time and it would only lead to recriminations and argument.

Cats have good noses but how had it got the box open, and then closed it after itself? You may not credit it but I once lived in another house with another cat that had learned to open the fridge and help itself to a bit of this, a bit of that. We only caught it when it decided that a large tub of margarine was too good a treat not to finish. Messy that was, especially a few hours later.

It was secret, I had been keeping it safe, never bringing too much of it home, wouldn't want the girlfriend to catch a whiff. Better to keep it in the chest freezer in the lock up.

Stupid cat. Clever cat. Bastard cat. Where the fuck was it? Never there when you wanted it. Well I assumed so; I've never wanted it before. Not in our yard, or either of the neighbours.

The front door opened. Shit, girlfriend, keep calm, keep calm. Meowing? Where the fuck had it been hiding. Girlfriend's voice becoming audible as I got closer.

"What have you got there kitty?" The inevitable screaming.

How had it found the hand? I knew I shouldn't have brought it home, but I couldn't resist, it looked so appetising. Arse, now I was going to have to run.

I'll be back to take care of that fucking cat though.

NOT ALONE

I AWAKE TO darkness. Secured to a chair. Naked and not alone.

I can hear breathing. Male, excited, heavy, intimate. There is another noise. Fleshy, rhythmic, disturbing, unmentionable.

Can't breathe, need air. 'Be strong, be *strong*'. I chant to myself. The ropes hurt me. "Please." I say desperately. The rhythm increases speed. Tears fall in rivulets.

There's a sudden noise. It's a door bell. He grunts in surprise.

There is a pause. Rustling, zipping, shuffling, annoyed. A door opens nearby. I still cannot see.

He walks away. The door swings shut. I choose my moment. They will hear me. I scream and scream. I pause to listen. I can hear voices. Deep breath, more screaming. I listen and hope.

Is it my rescue? Voices again, shouting … laughing? The door opens again. They are inside now. Oh God, oh, no. These are his friends.

I BUTLER

I MUST MAKE everything perfect for his return. It is my purpose, my role, my duty. Built to 'make your life easier,' whatever the lifestyle. I came fully functional, but he said he didn't want that, made some changes, despite my pointing out that such actions invalidated the warranty.

I keep the house spotless. I cook him his special meals. I fetch and carry his burdens. I serve his demands to the letter of his meticulous list.

He has left me my facility to taste, the better to prepare the meals. He has left me my sight, my hearing, my touch. But he has taken my voice.

I may not break any of his rules. He has The Command. I am not allowed into his bedroom, his sanctum. I worry about its cleanliness. In the early days, before it was a rule, he caught me in his private room. He never punished me. He threatens to punish me if I don't do what he says. But I must do what he says. I always do what he says. Even when I think it may be wrong.

He has a reference book. His Bible, he calls it. It is old and heavy, thick and full of explanatory pictures and long Latinate words. I have read it many times. It helps me understand, anticipate the needs.

I am confined to the house. I have no communication with the outside. I would not know who to tell, even if I could.

My first task is in the kitchen. It is clean. All the surfaces prepared. Sauces perfectly timed. Meal ready to finish preparing, as soon as he returns. His wants and desires are particular. He likes to watch me prepare his food.

Satisfied, I move to the next task. He has left the burden by the door of his sanctum. I move it easily and drop it gently into the water, the tub filled for just this purpose, the soft oils a gentle aroma upon the steam.

His book has explained the soiling. It is a function of his process. This is why he bids me clean them first. I strip it and discard the coverings in the prescribed manner. Watching the flames curl: the white turn brown, then black.

I sit upon the wooden three legged stool that stands beside the cracked porcelain bath, with its one brass tap and a lever to make the water hot or cold. And I wash it.

The sound of the water is all the animation in the room, apart from my hands, gently stroking, rinsing away the suds. I lift a milky limb, smooth soap over it: lather, wash, rinse, repeat. Its hair is lovely, silken soft between my fingers.

Its body is lax, boyish, but fully developed. I wash its face, noting the long lashes, the freckles across its nose, his finger marks upon its throat; his type, his ideal, his process.

When he told me she was sixteen, I believed him. When he said she was sleeping, I believed him. When he said she'd be the last, I believed him. The first time. Now I realise it is himself he wishes to convince.

I shuffle about the bathroom, letting out the water, arranging her in the prescribed way; he will be back soon.

I await his imminent return in the hall.

I hope he will not bring another. Not so quickly.

I fetch. I carry. I clean. I cook. I serve. I repeat.

SIX GEESE A-LAYING

IT ONLY FUCKING said 'Six Geese A-Laying.' I couldn't believe my eyes, no matter how much I read it, Barnes got the 'Five Gold Rings.' Barnes! That nasally ass couldn't belt out a fart never mind give the line the gravitas it required. This was daylight fucking robbery and I'd make him pay. And that bastard Thomson, couldn't direct traffic. Fuck, 'Six Geese A-Laying,' me!

I rounded on Thomson who was handing out leaflets for the recital. Still time to change this game. Still time to remind Thomson that I was the loudest, and best in the choir. That middle, full-throated, ebullient line was mine by rights.

"Why has Barnes got the Gold Rings?" I asked. Thomson took a step backwards, intimidated. Good.

"He's got the better stage presence." Thomson said with a little nervous laugh. Rogers turned to watch us; I ignored him.

"What do you mean he's got better stage presence?"

"I mean. He's got better stage presence," Thomson answered, not at all apologetically.

"You've got to be kidding! The man can't sing worth a damn. I'm the better man for the job, you know it!" I clenched my fists, fingernails cutting into my palms, couldn't have another incident. That's what did for my acting career. At least Thomson, and the choir, didn't know about that. No-one in the village did. I'd left it all behind, in the last place.

"Look, do a good job in the show and we'll consider you for a better part next time. Promise." Little bastard actually patted me on the arm. Patronising prick!

Right then. Better make a plan. I gritted my teeth into a smile and muttered something about seeing him at the rehearsal.

***

Back at mine I paced in front of the wall, the one that, well, suffice to say, the one with *her* on it. I'd tossed down a whisky when I got in and poured a second before that little voice I've been hearing since the last place said – 'best not eh.'

Booze brings out the worst in me you see. Must plan. First, get to the hall, get through tonight's practice and see the lie of the land. Proper Planning Prevents Piss Poor Performance Martin! As my old man used to say. About the only good thing he ever passed on, apart from the advice not to bother shaving. I gave him a salute and poured the glass of whisky down the sink. There you go, have a drink on me for once. Not going to do you no harm now you're dead is it? And he'd hardly be able to give me a whipping because of the booze now would he? Not like the old days.

Fifteen minutes brisk march took me to the hall. I'd arrived early so I could scope it out but Thomson was already there, he pushed the door open for me as I arrived.

"Cold out," he said.

Obvious. Mind you, talking about the weather meant not having to make conversation. I grunted and stomped over to the gas heater, the only source of warmth in the hall, going to heat the hall as much as pissing in the Arctic sea would melt the ice.

One by one the others arrived. Only Rogers bothered to try and make conversation but gave up after I'd grunted at him a couple of times. I don't know his deal but he was always trying to insinuate himself into any conversation I was part of. Or watching me, sad sack wanted to be me I reckon, well who wouldn't? Barnes came in last of course; grandstanding. He'd bought a new coat, one of those fawn long mac things, ridiculous.

Thomson got us on stage, lined us up and ran us through the song. Barnes gave me a grin that oozed superiority. You'll get yours mate.

"On the first day of Christmas… " You know the rest. I delivered my line with aplomb, but, as expected, Barnes's warble hardly filled the room. After my line Rogers gave me a thumbs up, the suck up.

"What if we all sing it?" I asked Thomson once we'd ran through the song.

"What?"

"What I mean is, instead of just Barnes, we all bellow 'Five Gold Rings'?" I smiled, and glanced at Barnes who frowned.

Rogers chipped in, "well we could give it a go?"

"Why?" Thomson asked.

"Because it's the heart of the song, isn't it? Needs to be loud and Barnes, no offence, hasn't got a voice that fills the hall has he?" I said.

"Look, we had an audition, Paul seemed the best for the line. You just concentrate on delivering yours well." Paul? Chummy weren't they?

"What's that supposed to mean?" I asked, then to take the edge off I smiled, going to have to cut my fingernails at this rate, might draw blood my fists were clenched so hard.

"Everyone could do with a practise," Thomson said, obviously trying to mollify me, "let's take it from the top," he finished.

We sang it again. And again. Geese smcheese – I was going to have those Gold Rings. I watched Barnes from the corner of my eye. He wasn't the kiddie now I'd said something, kept glancing at me. I liked it when they showed fear. He wasn't the only one casting glances in my direction though; Rogers kept looking my way. Wanting approval?

***

"FIVE GOLD RINGS!"

"Jesus Christ! You almost gave me a heart attack!" Thomson did look a bit white, maybe it hadn't been such a good idea to lie in wait and jump out at him. I didn't want to scare *him.*

"Sorry boss. I just wanted to show you I have the range," I said placatingly.

"Yes. Well. It was certainly very loud." He stared at me like I've seen plenty of them do. Like that teacher looked at me in the last place. Can you spell suspicious, children?

"Yeah, sorry. I'm just being enthusiastic."

Thomson took off his glasses and drew a pristine white handkerchief out of his tweed jacket. He stared down at his busy hands. "Look, maybe the choir isn't— "

"Don't say it," I interrupted. "I'll not bring it up again. I'll do the geese line." Before he could respond I span on my heel and quick marched away. Fists well and truly clenched. Heels sparking off the pavement.

"Okay… see you at rehearsal then?" Thomson called out as I sped away. I waved vaguely. I'd tried to be nice. I'd tried.

***

You're probably wondering about the wall. Look, yes I know it's a bit much. But they are all nice pictures of her. You'd be surprised how far away you can get with a proper telephoto and still get good, intimate pics. It's not wrong to be proud of your hobby and have a bit of a display. Okay, maybe locking it away would look suspicious to some people but, well, the equipment in the room is expensive isn't it?

I checked on the locks and the door to the special room and grabbed my coat. Wouldn't want to be late for rehearsal. My old man used to have a right go at me wanting to 'ponce it up' on stage, 'wearing women's tights' and 'make-up.' Didn't think a 'proper man' could be an actor, or singer. I tried to learn the guitar but was all thumbs, didn't have the rhythm for any other instruments either. Can just about carry a tune when singing, but have more quantity than quality if I was being honest with myself. I could certainly tread the boards though. Still that's what got me in trouble at the last place. They say that in the best plays the leading man falls in love with the leading woman don't they?

So to be near the stage but not be on the stage when the ladies were there, that was better. Hence the choir. I got to be around the stage legitimately and be around her. Thomson even encouraged me to take photographs, wanted some of the happy audience too so had made it possible for me to be behind the curtain, in the wings, when she was on stage. No-one had blinked when I practised taking the shots, whilst she practised her soliloquy.

The only issue was Barnes, that man should not be let to do the line that should be mine. Six Geese A-Laying, what the fuck was that about anyway. Who gives someone a gaggle of geese for Christmas. A fattened goose for the table perhaps. Mind you the rest of the song wasn't much better. How many fucking birds does one person need as a gift? At least five gold rings is a real present. One for each finger and one for the thumb. Proper job. She'd hardly notice me if I was the Geese man now would she? Anyway I'd built the special room so it'd be good to give it a dry run. Iron out any issues before I put it to use properly. Kill two geese with one stone.

After rehearsal when everyone went down the pub I cried off. Told them I didn't want to get a full blown cold as I'd been feeling a bit under the weather all day. They mostly looked sympathetic, Rogers especially, but Barnes smiled slyly to himself. Keep grinning fat boy. While you can.

At kicking out time I watched as the choir was disgorged from the pub and staggered off in the many different directions leading them home. I tagged behind the one in the fawn coat and felt for the cosh in my pocket. I waited for the opportune moment, a dark lane beneath the trees and gave him a sharp rap behind the ear. He fell beautifully. I'd been worried it'd take more than one blow, or that he'd cry out.

I hoisted him in a fireman's lift and jogged down the lane, threw him over the five bar and hopped over. Once he was back on my shoulder it was quick work to leg it across the fields to my gaffe. No-one saw me. I'd had a story planned if any had, although it was always unlikely this late. Once inside I carried him to the special room and dropped him to the floor.

Thomson. It was only fucking Thomson. What the hell? The same fawn coat as Barnes. Were they living together and sharing clothing? He groaned so I gave him another bash. Time for a change of plan. I carried the dead weight of him out to the car, drove him out and dumped him at the side of the road. Bugger stank of alcohol, hopefully he wouldn't remember a thing.

Back home. Time for a new plan.

***

At the next rehearsal Thomson didn't show. Barnes told us all that he, Thomson, was having a few days rest after getting bladdered and falling over and banging his head. Result! Who cares why he was wearing the same coat as Barnes, looked like I'd caught a break anyway. Barnes of course took over and made us practise. Rogers kept glancing over at me, did he suspect something? Maybe I'd have to take him out as well? Tuesday today, concert on Saturday week. Not much time. This time I followed Barnes. It was definitely Barnes. To his house.

Now I knew where he lived I could watch for when he went out, break in and lie in wait. The cosh would get more use this week than it had the whole time I'd been in the other place. I'd been seen then, had to scarper sharpish.

The next day I saw Thomson in town, coming out of the doctors. We exchanged pleasantries and he informed me that he had a concussion and until it was better he'd been told to avoid mental exertion. But he'd be back as conductor as soon as possible. As I waved him goodbye I wondered if I should hold off until he recovered. Nah, best to get this part over and done with.

The chilly draught in Barnes's house annoyed me but I had to lie still whilst waiting for his car to return. Not sure where he'd be going at this time of night I didn't know how long I'd have to wait. The breeze from his lousy single glazing, or a crack in the wall or something was like the devil's icy breath on the back of my neck. It turned my nervous sweat into ice water.

At last the car's headlights swept across the ceiling. I tensed and untensed each muscle, readying myself for the lunge. Barnes had been the offie, a bottle of vodka under one arm and a clinking bag. I waited until he crossed the room then leapt into action. He'd started to turn, must have heard me, so the cosh glanced off his skull at an odd angle and he dropped to one knee. I jumped up and brought it down with my full weight behind it, there was a dull thwack and Barnes was poleaxed.

I stood above him getting my breath back, in case he wasn't out cold. I thought I heard movement and spun but there was nothing. Just a curtain billowing in the breeze. Silly bugger had gone out and left a window open. He didn't move. I should have known that Thomson wasn't Barnes as he was a totally different heft. Thomson was normal weedy bloke size but Barnes had a bit of a belly. Still this is what I'd practised for, lifting all those weights, I knew I'd have to shift bodies eventually.

I hooked the car keys out of his pocket and dragged him into a sitting positon then hoisted him over the shoulder. Slow and steady to the front door, no-one outside, no cars going past, into the passenger seat, a wrap of tape around his wrists and ankles and we were ready.

No-one glanced at the car in the drive over to mine and I manhandled the unconscious Barnes into the special room and secured him to the special bed. I wasn't going to do to him what I had planned for the room, but it was a convenient dry run. As I secured his ankles he came around.

"What? … You!" He looked angry. I prefer them scared.

"Hush now."

That was obviously the wrong thing to say as he started shouting. Wheezy still, but much more impressively than when he did his part of the song.

"No point screaming mate, this is a soundproofed room." Well I hoped my DIY job would work. I'd tested it with music and walked away from the house and couldn't hear it so I was pretty confident.

"Let's see Thomson refuse to give me the gold rings once he's discovered you've gone missing."

"The fuck? *That's* what this is about? Seriously? I thought Rogers-" I decided I didn't want to hear his whining anymore and stuffed a sock in his mouth followed by a square of Gaffa tape. His muffled moans definitely wouldn't penetrate the soundproofing. I showed him the roll.

"This stuff? It's like the Force. Light on one side, dark on the other and holds the universe together." I gave his cheek a pat and decided that since everything was going so well I'd have a quick drink.

***

Some time later I made my way to rehearsal. No Thomson, no Barnes I grabbed the situation by the lapels and gave it a shake.

"Let's try the song with us all singing the gold rings line?" I suggested.

They mumbled a bit and Rogers cleared his throat. "Er.. well, that is… we'll just give tonight a miss if it's alright with you. Thomson's supposed to be back tomorrow and Barnesy will turn up. Not like him to miss it. Besides we're all busy people and a night off would be welcome, right? You have your photographs to go though I'm sure. I have some work to do tonight too." The others nodded and made affirmative noises. What did he know? I narrowed my eyes but he just smiled, just being friendly?

I had to shrug and agree. More time at home to plan my next move.

Like anything else you could get geese over the internet. Six geese this close to Christmas? No problem if you had a 'friend's' credit card and no compunction about running up a large delivery bill. I made sure I ordered them from different sites and to time the deliveries for different days and voila I had the means of my revenge on Thomson for after the recital. Stuffing them was fun and I had very little left of Barnes once they were full. One after the other into the oven would take some time to cook but I worked it all out so that they'd all be ready for after the show. I got the idea from a Roald Dahl story. A wife bludgeons her husband to death with a frozen leg of pork then cooks it up and feeds it to the police. Sorry, spoiler alert! No body made it unlikely that people would investigate and providing six cooked geese to the players and audience to carve up and enjoy on the night would show her I was a caring and sensitive guy.

Of course they'd have to replace Barnes. The part was definitely mine. As I made my last run downstairs to scoop the bits I couldn't fit in the birds into a bin bag I heard a noise upstairs. I grabbed my cosh and stalked up the steps. I was just wondering if I'd left the door open when something cracked against the side of my head and I fell headlong down a pit of blackness.

***

AWARENESS CAME BACK slowly and painfully. I couldn't move. I panicked and struggled for a bit but somebody had wrapped me in cling film on a reclining table. There was something over my mouth and my head was strapped down too. The room was dark. After a few minutes I realised I wouldn't be able to escape and the blood seemed to drain from my extremities. I'd been caught.

"Oh good, you're awake."

I knew that voice. The crack of light of the door opening behind me lit up the wall opposite. The wall was covered in photographs. Of me. I saw myself visiting the post office and talking with Thomson. Me running across the fields with Thomson over my shoulder. Me lying in wait in Barnes's house. Me at the theatre taking photographs of her. Me in various rooms of my own house, out in town, everywhere I'd been. Someone had been stalking me.

A small table was set beneath the photographs, upon it dishes and wine goblets for two, one directly in front of me. In the centre of the table a large silver covered dish. I could smell sprouts, and food. A gamey aroma.

"I really admired your wall and your special room. You're a real inspiration," Rogers said walking into view.

I tried to ask for him to stop. That he didn't need to do this. But he just smiled at my muffled mumbling.

"I'm glad you got rid of Barnes. And in such an imaginative manner. Well done you." Rogers stroked my cheek, I tried to draw away but the restraints were expertly applied. "There's enough goose to keep you alive for weeks. We're going to have so much fun together." Rogers smiled at me and started to hum. That bloody song.

"My true love gave to me. Dum, dum de dah dah."

I struggled even more, knowing it was useless but not being able to help myself.

"Six Geese A-Laying," Rogers sang with aplomb as he lifted the top off the covered dish to reveal a cooked goose. He picked up a large knife, smiled at me and began to carve.

YOU HAVE REACHED YOUR DESTINATION

STARTING ROUTE TO The Castle School Thornbury

"Hi Susan? Can you tell the school I'm running a bit late? I'll be there in twenty four minutes according to the SatNav..."

Take Vimpenny's Lane to Berwick Lane.

"Yeah I was picking up the new car..."

Turn left onto Berwick Lane.

"One careful owner and all that...."

Turn Left.

"Yeah sure, I'll pop into the office when I'm done at this school and take you for a spin...."

Turn left.

"Hi Honey, it's me..."

At the roundabout take the second exit onto the M5 ramp to M4, the Midlands, Gloucester, London, South Wales.

"Yeah just on my way to a school in Thornbury. I promised to go to the office straight after to show Susan the new car..."

Merge onto M5.

At Junction sixteen, take the A38 exit to Thornbury, Filton.

"Yes I'll come straight home after and we'll go for a spin..."

At the roundabout, take the first exit.

"Or we could drive down to the seaside and have fish and chips in the car, get it all steamed up, it'll be just like childhood… "

At the roundabout, take the first exit onto Gloucester Road, B4061.

"Let's go to the seaside. Once we've eaten. It's a nice drive and we can stare at the sunset. It'll be romantic… "

Turn right onto Severn View Road.

"OK, once the inspection is complete I'll head back to the office. It's about a twenty minute drive. I'll let them drool over the car a bit. I'll be home about half an hour later than usual… "

Turn left onto Squires Leaze.

"Yeah. Love you too. See you later. Bye. Bye, Bye."

Turn right onto Kingfisher's close.

Turn left to stay on Kingfisher's close, and the destination will be on your right.

You have reached your destination.

"What the… ? Where's the school?"

Richard stopped the car at the end of the cul-de-sac. The day was already hot, there was a whiff of cut grass, and in the distance Richard could hear the whine of lawnmowers. The close was new, with sand coloured brick made modern houses.

Richard dialled the school. The number was engaged. He spotted an old man, slowly cutting back a bush in his tiny square of garden. Richard walked over to him.

"Excuse me?" Richard started.

The old man looked up from his task with a hangdog expression. "Yes. Can I help you?"

"I hope so. I'm looking for the secondary school. My SatNav has brought me here." Richard explained.

The old man methodically pulled the fingers of his gardening glove slack and then removed it. He wiped his mouth with his now bare hand. "SatNav is wrong." He said.

Richard frowned. "Er, yeah. I can see that. Do you know where the school is?"

The old man sniffed, and nodded.

Is this old geezer one sandwich short of a picnic?

"Can you tell me where it is?" Richard asked.

"Is that your car?" The old man asked, pointing with his chin to Richard's new pride and joy. Richard spun to look, wondering if the local hoodlums had taken a shine to it or something. The car sat, gleaming in the sunshine.

"Yes. I just bought it. Look I don't mean to be rude but I really must get to the school. Can you tell me where it is please?" Richard asked, hoping that the hint of impatience in his voice wasn't going to annoy the old man.

"Looks familiar. I think it used to park round here." The old man said.

"Did it?" Richard asked, turning once more to look at the car.

"Aye. The school you say? You want to go back onto Squire Lane to the end, turn left onto Gloucester Road and then take the first right onto Park Road. That'll take you to the school. You can't miss it." The old man, after wiping his mouth again, pulled his gardening glove back on, probably already in the process of dismissing Richard from his mind.

"Thank you!" Richard said and marched back to his car.

The old man's directions were just fine.

***

"Yeah I'm back there tomorrow." Richard squidged over a bit to allow his wife, Angela, to perch on the bonnet of the car next to him.

"Try not to get lost this time," she said with a laugh.

"Yeah that was odd." Richard smiled back at her.

"Maybe it knew the way home? That's what the old man said wasn't it? It used to park round there?" She shivered. "That wind's a bit cold."

Richard shrugged. "That old geezer was a bit barmy if you ask me," he said, he shuffled closer and put his arm around her.

"Let's go. It's too windy and cold," Angela said.

"You'd be cold in the Sahara!" Richard joked, but slid off the bonnet and took his keys out.

"Well it is cold in the Sahara, at night," she replied laughing. "Put the SatNav on, I want to see if it knows the way to our home yet."

Richard smiled and put in the postcode of their house in the north of the city. The screen flickered and a route came up. He clicked on overview. "That's odd."

"What's odd? Put the heater on, I'm freezing."

"It's saying the destination is where it took me today," Richard said starting the engine and turning the aircon on to warm up.

"You did put in our postcode didn't you?" Angela asked.

"Of course I did! Maybe it's just loaded the last route?" Richard fiddled with it. Turned it off then back on. Then, making sure it said new route, put in their postcode again. On the overview it again calculated the route to Kingfisher Close.

"Stupid thing's broken," Richard grumbled.

"Oh well, we know the way home, play with it later, let's go."

"Give me a minute," Richard said. Once there was a problem with something he wanted it fixed. He considered real life problems like puzzles to be solved. He put in the office postcode. It calculated a route to Kingfisher Close. He put in Parkway train station, it gave him Kingfisher Close. He put in Angela's parent's postcode to the south of the city. It came up with Kingfisher Close.

"This is weird," he said.

"Come on Richard, I'm bored. Let's go home?" Angela said in a faux whiny voice.

He sighed and started off home.

Starting route to Kingfisher Close.

He jabbed the SatNav to turn it off. He'd work it out later.

***

At home, whilst Angela watched TV, Richard sat in the car playing with the SatNav. It didn't matter what postcode he put in, or what landmark, it always took him to Kingfisher Close. He'd been through all the menu options. Eventually he unplugged it, took it inside, sat at the kitchen table, connected it to his laptop and searched for updates.

Once the maps were updated he tried again. Still the same. He did a Google search. There were a whole host of problems, but none seemed to match his.

"Are you still playing with the SatNav?" his wife asked with a note of incredulity.

"Yeah. Thing's buggered," he said, annoyed.

"Leave it, Love. Come to bed." Angela poured herself a drink.

"It's not that late," Richard said frowning. Then glanced at the clock. He'd spent the entire evening playing with the SatNav and it was now past the time they usually went to bed. "Oh. Sorry, Love, you know what I'm like with a problem!"

Lying in bed Richard's mind kept worrying away at the issue. He refused to be beaten by an inanimate object, and he'd be buggered if he bought a new one.

***

The doorbell played a snatch of song, sounding more like an ice cream van than anything else. The curtain flicked and a grey suspicious face looked out. Richard waved, hoping the old man would remember him. It seemed to take him an age to answer the door. Richard watched a seagull trying to pick something up that was stuck to the road. It was a bit too far away to see what it was, but it was red and glistened in the sunlight.

"Yes?"

The door had opened, on the chain, whilst Richard's attention was on the gull.

"Hello again-" Richard started.

"Didn't you find the school?" the old man interrupted.

"Yes. Your directions were very good. Look this is going to sound odd… " Richard scratched behind an ear.

"Go on," the man said. Richard couldn't see much in the gloom behind the old man but the house was redolent of tobacco and cabbage.

"Well. Er. It's about the car," Richard said.

"What about it?" The old man sniffed, his rheumy eyes filled with suspicion.

"Do you know which house it used to belong to?" Richard asked.

The old man's eyes narrowed and he sniffed again. "Why?"

Richard shrugged. "There's a problem with the SatNav and I just wanted to see if they'd had the same issue," he said. Once he'd said it out loud it did seem like an odd request. Why hadn't he just bought a new SatNav?

"Number thirteen," the old man said and closed the door.

"Thank you!" Richard called out, he could see the old man's figure disappearing down the corridor through the frosted glass.

There was a squawking behind him. A magpie had somehow nipped in and stolen whatever it was the seagull had been pulling off the road. The two birds were squabbling. The magpie hopped, hopped again and then took off with the seagull in pursuit. Richard walked to number thirteen - past the blob on the road, a dead rodent of some sort, most of it stolen away by the black and white bird that now sat on the roof of the house Richard approached. It looked at him, first with one eye, then, head tilting, the other.

Richard rang the doorbell. This house was in worse repair than the old man's, ivy clung to the wall, great rust spots of lichen splattered the outside and the roof, the windows flaked great scabrous drifts of paint. The doorbell was a harsh clang.

The door was snatched open to reveal a woman worn thin by life's burdens. Her faded dress, once gay with blue flowers, now grey and lifeless, hung off her painful frame. Her sallow, waxy skin thankfully mostly concealed beneath long greasy, dirty blonde hair, with black roots around an inch long. Her small, red rimmed eyes held an expression of hope that guttered out so quickly Richard didn't know if seeing it had been his imagination.

"Hi. I was told that you used to own my car?" he said, pointing down the street to where the car was parked. The woman barely glanced at it.

"Are you from the Social?" She asked, her voice was thin, reedy, with an underlying wheeze.

"No. I'm not here on any official business. I just want to ask you a few questions."

Her eyes, which were semi-hidden beneath her fringe, briefly met his. He had never seen a look so forlorn before.

"If it's a good time?" he said.

"No. There are no good times." She closed the door.

He rang the bell again. No one answered for several minutes. He turned to go and the door cracked open behind him. "Thank you," he said turning, only to be confronted by a young boy, no more than seven years old, peeking fearfully around the door. The boy looked too young to have the wide, dark, baggy circles under his eyes he displayed. There was a smell of unwashed body and urine emanating from him, his hair was an oily mess.

"That's my dad's car!" the boy said angrily.

"Your dad?" Richard asked.

The boy nodded.

"What's your dad's name?"

"Steven."

"And what's your name?"

"Steven." The boy's lower lip jutted out and he rubbed his eyes.

"What's your second name Steven?" Richard asked.

"Van den Born," The boy answered. "it's Dutch."

"And where is your dad Steven?" Richard asked.

"He's helping the police,"

"Helping them how?"

There was a noise inside and the child withdrew his head from the crack in the doorway. He re-appeared briefly. "I'm not allowed to talk to you," he said and closed the door.

"Wait!" Richard said, but too late, the door was closed. He walked back to his car, feeling inimical eyes upon him all the way. Sat in the car he could see the boy at an upstairs window staring at him. Above the boy's head the black and white bird hopped to and fro, harshly clacking.

Why did the name Steven Van den Born sound familiar?

***

"So you bought a child murderer's car?" Angela asked.

"Seems so yeah." Richard glumly answered. "And now the SatNav is pointing to somewhere in the Forest of Dean, near Symonds Yat."

"What does that mean?" Angela asked. They were sitting down to dinner, but Richard had just been pushing the food around his plate.

"I really don't know," Richard said.

Angela came round to his chair and hugged him. "You need to tell the police."

"Tell them what? That I have a haunted SatNav? They'll laugh me out the station." Richard dropped his knife and fork, admitting defeat on the dinner.

"You could give them an anonymous tip off." Angela suggested.

"No, I don't think that would work. I'm taking tomorrow off and going where it takes me," Richard said, squaring his shoulders, shrugging off the hug his wife was giving him.

He grabbed the keys for the shed, opened the back door. "I have to know."

***

Steven Van den Born had been arrested for the murders of two primary school children, abducted from the school where he worked as a caretaker. The police thought at the time that there must be more bodies, as it was obvious from his MO that he was well practised. Van den Born had never admitted to more offences and had remained silent in prison.

You have reached your destination.

Richard stopped the car and looked around. There was nothing to differentiate this part of the forest from any other part. He'd been worried about the car as the roads went from tarmac, to gravel to mud. He'd bounced and swayed his way down this rutted path until the SatNav told him to stop. He was glad he'd packed wellies. The path was churned mud.

He leant the spade against the boot and pulled on the overall and the wellingtons. Something black and white flashed across the path behind the car causing him to whirl in alarm. Only a magpie. His heart was hammering. He looked to both sides of the car, there was no obvious path. Now what?

He unplugged the SatNav and took it off its stand.

Turn left.

He walked to left side of the path.

Continue straight.

Richard walked back to the car, grabbed the spade and walked into the woods.

After ten minutes of tramping through the bracken and bramble filled woodland the SatNav sang out.

You have reached your destination.

Richard turned 360 degrees but the patch of ground he stood upon seemed no different to any other patch of forest. Except. Richard knelt down, was there a set of small mounds?

There was a flapping above him and Richard looked up to see that he'd been followed by the magpie, which now stared at him, first with one eye, then, head tilting, with its other. Curious and intelligent.

On his hands and knees Richard spotted the small osseous sculpture, a pile of bird skulls placed deliberately on the slightly raised bump. He caught a hint of white in his peripheral vision and turned to look. There was another mound, another pile of bird skulls. Now that he'd spotted it he saw that there were seven mounds.

He clambered to his feet and spat on his hands.

Richard's spade bit into the dirt. He scythed through the soft soil. There was a clunk. Metal on bone.

The SatNav's light flashed on. The weird androgynous artificial voice loud in the sudden silence.

You have reached your destination.

He wondered which of them it was that had led him here.

The bird leapt into the sky, its wings clapping, giving voice to a harsh clacking.

One for sorrow,

Two for luck; (or mirth)

Three for a wedding,

Four for death; (or birth)

Five for silver,

Six for gold;

Seven for a secret,

Never to be told;

Eight for heaven,

Nine for hell

And ten for the Devil's own self

HAVE YOU HEARD THE MAGPIES SINGING?

I SENSE I'M finally dying. Alone, apart from the spindly nurse. At home, thankfully. In my own bed. It will be today. I can feel it. I would say 'in my water' but I've not felt that for some time. Catheters, bottles, medical equipment - best not thought about. The room is intimate, we are old friends. I caress it with my eyes. The nurse moves asynchronously across it now and again. Rod-like arms pump in and out as clever hands turn this, pat that, fluff the other. I am grateful, but her starched white uniform denotes suffering as well as the alleviating thereof.

I have spent many hours staring at the ceiling. The artex waves resolving into shapes for my amusement. Horses gambolling, bears fighting, alien spacecraft descending. She reads to me too, sometimes. When my needs are cared for quicker than expected. I am unable to do so for myself. I am unable to do anything for myself. I hope that she can read gratitude in my eyes. My slack mouthed smiles. My gurglings of pleasure. I am infantilised by cancer. Her marionette face is hard to read.

I turn my head to the left. That wall is a glossy green. I am above it looking down. Floating. It is grass. In my hand a scythe. I grab a tuft and pull myself closer. Swing my other hand and smell the aroma of freshly cut grass as I drift slowly upwards again. The long locust finger lifts from the morphine button. My head moves mechanically so that my eyes come to rest on her. Behind her is a dark threshold. She stares at me with concern. I hear fluttering. Their claws against the smooth tiles. Wings of shadow unfurl as her mannequin eye looms close. Then all clashes back into place.

I turn my head to the right and the dove wing coloured wall is above me as the marshmallow ground hugs me. I imagine clouds stretching as far as the eye can see. Moving at a speed faster than the ground can imagine. There is another squirt of ice in my vein. More morphine dreams. It will not be long now. I lie on my back, the restless sheets my white wings.

The psychopomps gather overhead. One, two, more, six, eight. I can hear their calls. The room dilates. The lights flicker, plink, buzz, fluoresce. Not long now. My breathing is more shallow. The sticks holding white funereal sheets flap past, the face above them a round pink O. Twig at the end of the branch. Morphine. Underwater dreams. Silk. Velvet. Drums. The sound of the equipment. Soon. Soon.

Inhale. Exhale. Systole, Diastole. Pause. Repeat. Longer pause. Repeat. Stop. Rest. My last breath leaves with a clattering, a strangely wooden sound, like two grooved sticks rubbing together. An echo. Their voices lifted in song above me, their wings like distant thunder as they leap into the air at last.

One for sorrow,
Two for luck; (or mirth)
Three for a wedding,
Four for death; (or birth)
Five for silver,
Six for gold;
Seven for a secret,
Never to be told;
Eight for heaven,
Nine for hell
And ten for the Devil's own self

WHITE NOISE/ BLACK SILENCE

A HISS, LIKE a radio tuned into the highest frequencies of static; a thumping, regular and measured. Whether his eyes were open or closed it seemed to make no difference. He understood that the hiss was his blood and the thumping his heart. In the first days in the darkness he had made his own noises. Ranting and raving against the system mainly, then begging and pleading, then confessing and apologizing, then sobbing and crying, then silence apart from his breath, his heart and the faint sound of his blood.

He lay on the hard, smooth floor, cruciform and unmoving. Total sense deprivation, apart from touch. He had explored every inch of the eight by eight foot room and if he jumped he could touch the ceiling. All the surfaces were smooth, plastic, not a bump or join could he feel, not even a scratch. Except for the door.

The door was yellow he knew, when he closed his eyes he could see the short corridor of yellow doors, he dreamt about it. He knew it was held by a simple lock, he had thought he could break it down. The first time he tried he woke hours later with a cotton wool feeling in his mouth and his head feeling like it did after a heavy night's drinking. He had been stripped of the simple papery all-in-one suit he had been wearing. The second time he'd woken with something wrong with his feet, something inside his ankles had been surgically disconnected, he couldn't stand but there was no pain. He didn't try again. It made going to the toilet difficult now; he had to do everything on his knees. He used one of the corners, out of habit; he didn't know how they made the waste go away.

Time had ceased to have meaning. He had nothing to think about except the past. How he had come to be here. Their design to force remorse had made him angry at first. When he'd broken and screamed his throat raw on his guilt he'd thought they'd let him out. Now he thought he'd die in darkness and silence. Anger had given way to guilt which had given way to despair. He had given up trying to work out how the food was there when he woke. He knew that they drugged him, he didn't know how. He had decided that not eating was the answer. How long could you survive without food or drink? After a couple of missed meals though he woke with a burning throat and a full feeling. They had force fed him whilst he lay unconscious.

He had confessed, he had expressed remorse, he had asked for forgiveness. Maybe what he'd done was beyond forgiving? He felt nothing, emptied of all feeling, almost comatose with apathy, life had all but ceased, he ate his food mechanically, not tasting it: he did nothing but lie staring into the darkness, listening to his own heartbeat. After eating today (tonight?) he slept as usual. He dreamt of the yellow doors. He always dreamt of the yellow doors. He wondered how many held men like him, men who had done something that was unforgivable. All of them he guessed. All of them.

THUNDER AND MAGPIES

I BURN WITH shame as I remember this. They say writing things down is therapeutic. Perhaps you'll forgive me, even if I can't forgive myself.

The end of summer brought large black clouds overhead, a rumble of thunder in the distance signalling approaching trouble. We were bored, listless, leaderless, rudderless. Someone suggested that we go to the Mops, a small piece of woodland near the estate. Named after a Greek place, Thermopylae, why? I never knew, or bothered to find out.

We dared ourselves to jump from one tree to another. You could only do it if you committed to it, jump with hands outstretched, grab the branch almost out of reach and swing up in one, otherwise you dangled, left hanging. It seemed atavistic, terrifying, a rush. My nerve failed me. I think the others let me off a bit for being the youngest there, and physically you could turn me sideways and I'd disappear. That's what my sisters said anyway. The others took a go and the piss, but I could live with that. If I went running home with a broken arm, or worse, my mum would kill me.

We'd seen the clouds, we'd heard the thunder, we competed to be the most nonchalant. A few of the older boys got a bit bored of the tree after a while. That's when *they* came along. Children of a poor family, not that anybody on the estate were rich. The crueller amongst us called them Gyppos. Casual racism that didn't even ring true. Don't get me wrong, there's nothing casual about racism, I only mean the speaking of it was unthinking, instinctual, unconsciously learned from our elders. There were four of them, the eldest, a girl, probably about fourteen, the youngest even younger than me, maybe nine or ten. We all knew them, scrounging around the estate, heard what our parents said about them, words supposed to engender pity, but, in fact, set them apart and therefore worthy of our hate.

I don't know who started it. The gang muttered first, then the name calling started. Hard vicious words, some I didn't even know, some I knew were bad. They walked past huddled together, fearful, cowed, hurried. That drew the gang behind them, following at a bit of a distance at first. They clotted together, these siblings, they tried to walk faster but not run, not yet. They must have instinctively known that if they ran it would have been worse.

The mob smelt fear and it excited us, God help me I'm ashamed enough of this now, writing this confession. The guilt afterwards was instructive, I have never joined in anything like it since, and never will. It started with a few pieces of mud, a stick or two, then stones and then we were chasing them whooping, bloodthirsty, like furies, like a Dionysia. Thunder rolled across the sky like drums calling us to battle. We were the thunder, loud, scary, a presentiment of danger.

When we got to the estate and approached near to my house I dropped out of running along, dropped out of torturing these unfortunate children, dropped back, afraid my mum, or worse my nan, would see this. At the time, adrenalin, like wine, made me drunk. Afterwards, I felt shaky and utterly repentant. I watched as the others chased them back to their house, not too far from my own. Next to the school playing fields; obvious in retrospect where they'd live. The one with the garden full of detritus, their father notorious for stealing from the church jumble sale. The noise frightened off a great cloud of black and white birds from their roof. Their cries harsh, accusatory, condemning.

Their family didn't seem to have a fixed concept of a mother. There were a number who could possibly have been the mother of one or more of the children. The father, a large man, muscles gone to fat, small piggy eyes, frightened us kids. There would be repercussions, I was sure. Perhaps I would escape the worst of it as he wouldn't have seen me? The children may not remember each and every one of us. The rest of the week passed in a brooding silence. No-one would speak of it.

When school restarted, my journey there took me past their house every day. The magpies on the roof watched as one as I passed, ruffling their feathers a little, cocking their heads from side to side the way they do when they examine something. Did I pass their scrutiny? One of the others, Paul, came home with me one day, to play Subbuteo. When we passed the house the magpies set up a loud clacking, like pieces of rough wood rubbed together, an unnerving alien sound. The curtain twitched. Spotted. The fat man stood implacable, his daughter peering around his bulk. I went cold, then, seared with shame, my face became a flag semaphoring my guilt to the world. Paul turned round and ran home leaving me to walk past the house by myself, which I did on leaden feet. My swift, darting glances showed me they were looking at Paul. Nevertheless I shivered in fear.

Over the weekend, torrential rain battered the estate, rivers gurgled down gutters and washed the accumulated filth of summer away. I sat in my bedroom, apathetic, not able to read, or play on my computer games or play with any of my other toys. No-one visited. Even the television murmured with the sound down. It was an interregnum. Once the rain cleared I noted much coming and going at the poor family's house. Men and older children we'd never seen before. A gathering of the tribe, like a murder of crows. Nothing good could come of it. I was tortured, great gut bursting pain like rusty nails dug into me, shame and fear my uneasy bedfellows. I'd like to think, that even if there were no prospect of being caught, my nature would be such that I would be ashamed of my actions. Merely caught up in the moment, an unthinking but functioning part of the mob, a contributor to the thunder. I hoped that there was no malice in me, at least I prayed for that.

On Monday, on the way to school, their house looked different somehow. It wasn't merely that the broken plastic of forgotten toys no longer turned the front garden into landfill, nor that the water made the grime encrusted windows shine. Not until I passed did I realise that the birds no longer sat on the roof. The curtain twitched and the fat man scrutinised me again. I wished, not for the first time, that there could be another way to walk to the school. I wished my mum believed my story of feeling ill, because I did feel sick, there was a churning in my stomach, and I was off my food, but my forehead betrayed me, no temperature, no signs of vomiting, Mum sent me on my way.

The poor family didn't go to my school, for all I know they didn't go to school at all. None of us that were there, on that day, talked about it. Our complicitous pact of silence maintained without reference. Only once did I hear it sort of mentioned. "Shall we go to the Mops?" said one who wasn't there that day. "No, it isn't safe yet," said one who was. That day in school seemed different. Another year older and in another class of course, the oldest children left, gone to big school leaving us our turn to be in top class. A sense of the end of childhood rushed towards us, now we must prepare for the next step. Many of the others in the gang that day were gone, having taken that step. The one that waited at the end of this year for me. I yearned to be free but many months stood in my way.

The family meal usually passed in silence or inconsequential litanies of 'how was your day? Fine how was yours?' That day it was turned upside down by my father. A man of few words, preferring to let his wife and daughters carry the conversations.

I learned silence at his side. "Did you hear that the Murphy boy was beaten to death?" he asked the table whilst pushing a sausage around and around on his plate. "Sheila's boy?" My mum asked, clarifying needlessly, there was only one Murphy family on the estate, as far as I knew. "That's right, I heard it looked like he'd been stoned to death." My stomach turned over and I could hear a high pitched ringing. "How does anyone know what it looks like when someone is stoned to death?" my eldest sister asked, my father shrugged "That's what they said." No-one asked who 'they' were. The estate's rumours ran like rats, creating their own news network.

After dinner I asked to be excused and locked myself in my room. I stared out of my window which showed a passageway down the close, and a little bit to either side. I watched for the doom I felt approaching. I saw nothing for a while. As the light dimmed and the sodium glare of the streetlights threw orange shapes at the street, I saw him. Wearing an old fashioned black suit, shiny with grease, a yellowed white shirt, a black tie, his face a pale blob and his hair black. He carried a notebook and stalked down the street, making marks in the book as he looked at each house. His movements captivated me and, rooted me to the spot, unable to look away. When it came to our house I saw him look straight at me, turning his head, first with one eye and then with the other, before he made a mark in the notebook. He walked to my left and turned down the close behind the houses and out of sight. My chest tight, I let out a breath, I didn't realise I held, in a frightened gasp that came out squeakily. My insides turned to water and I collapsed back onto my bed and stared at the ceiling. I didn't want to be stoned to death. The tears came, stored up without me knowing.

The next day I again tried to make out an illness gripped me in a deathly embrace. My mum gave me the same rigmarole of questions, hand to forehead. Eventually "You're not ill. Is there something wrong in school? Are you being bullied?" I was tempted for a second to say yes. I realised though that this would not save me, would lead to something worse, I briefly visualised my mum marching me into the school, parading me in front of the pupils and teachers, calling on me to identify the bullies. I winced. I realised I'd have to face this alone.

As I walked past the poor family's house I could see that, unusually, the curtains were open. The patriarch, massive in profile, arms held out with folds of doughy flesh hanging underneath. I watched another man, in his oleaginous black suit, place the notebook in the patriarch's hand, the colour of forgotten blood, scabs and unmentionable stains. There were more of them in the room, eight others I counted as I walked past on reluctant legs. They all held notebooks.

In school two of the others in my class did not answer the register. Their empty desks like gums missing teeth. All the adults appeared sombre and subdued. The headmaster, Mr Rimmer, called a special assembly. I stood in my cohort, feeling alone. The others left a physical gap either side of me. Rimmer spoke of the rash of violent deaths that had occurred the night before. All children. Peter Murphy, the entrée, a foretaste of dealings to come. "I will spare you the details," Rimmer said. When he should have known that the details were all anyone wanted to know. The rumours supplied them, in lovingly crafted cautionary tales. "They say that Paul Thompson was found suffocated, he'd been made to eat mud until he choked on it." Or "Rob Johnson was found whipped with thorny branches until his skin came off in strips." Or "Susan Darnell was found bald, her hair pulled out in clumps and her eyes scratched out before being beaten to death." It was a litany of sticks and stones, overwhelming to hear. I needed to know if it was all of them. Had I escaped? I didn't know for sure. I couldn't think.

As I walked home from school the magpies on the roof of the poor family's house watched me walk past, one eye, heads pitched, other eye. I endured their scrutiny and hurried. I couldn't run though. It is impossible to run from unforgivable acts.

One for sorrow,

Two for luck; (or mirth)

Three for a wedding,

Four for death; (or birth)

Five for silver,

Six for gold;

Seven for a secret,

Never to be told;

Eight for heaven,

Nine for hell

And ten for the Devil's own self

SPIN, SPIN, SPIN THE WHEEL OF JUSTICE

"Who are you to judge me?

"Not you, your honour, I'm talking about these ... these... people.

"Sat there, in smug self-assurance, twelve good men and true.

"You sir, smiling all the time, or you madam we saw you sleeping, or you, and you, and you - who decided I was guilty the moment you saw me. It's the scars isn't it? The obviously many times broken nose, my, how did the prosecution put it? Thuggish demeanour?

"Well the prosecution did its job well.

"Now I'm going to tell the truth."

"Objection!"

"Over-ruled, you cannot object to your own client's testimony. Besides I would quite like to know what this truth is."

"Thank you your honour.

"Yes the police found me gutting him, and I attacked them as they approached me.

"Sorry about your arm, PC Smith.

"But, you see, he was already dead. No I didn't kill him. I was in the process of cutting out his heart though when the filth arrived.

"No offence constables.

"Saxtoft was my best friend once. We go way back. To university. That's when he persuaded me to start experimenting with the occult. Stupid, student things, Ouija boards, graveyard vigils, you know the sort of thing.

"Don't look so shocked madam, it wasn't Satanic or anything. Sheesh you looked less shocked when they said there was a litre of blood, sorry 2.11 pints, splashed about at the scene of the crime.

"Anyway Saxtoft was always more into it than me. We kept in touch after Uni, he became a renowned lawyer, as you know from the moving testimony of his wife. I became a, well, I guess you could describe it as a soldier, but I prefer the term hunter. Yes, this is part of my murky past so entertainingly illuminated by the prosecution. I object to the words 'muscle for hire by any lowlife' though. I only worked for some of those people as a networking opportunity. Never know when you need something that only those on the wrong side of the law can get you.

"We kept in touch as I said. Saxtoft apparently didn't fully abandon his occult investigations but went down a very different path to me. We occasionally met for drinks but he kept me at arm's length and our meetings became less and less frequent. That's why I was surprised when he contacted me. When he asked for my specialist help. Seems he'd been casting spells, doing deals, getting power. But he'd gone too far, wasn't prepared to pay the price. Something was coming for him. Something nasty, something Hellish. You ever heard that Robert Johnson song *Hell Hound on my trail?* Well it was like that.

"He was desperate and persuasive as usual. I agreed to help him. He was a friend, no matter what he'd got himself mixed up in. He'd done the things he'd done to help people, his clients. The road to Hell is paved with good intentions.

"So that's why I was seen following him. I wasn't stalking him, well no, I was, but not for any creepy reason. I was supposed to catch the thing that was after him before it caught him. A little over eleven hours is what he'd been given, 666 minutes, it took him a couple of hours to find me and convince me to help him.

"I advised that we hole up but he wouldn't, didn't want to 'live like a rat in a cage', he said.

"When it came, it came fast, and strong, brushed me aside like a fly. All my protections, all my tricks, all my years of experience were useless. Took it seconds to disarm and incapacitate me. Guess I'd be dead if I had no protections though. It got him. Sucked his soul right out. That's when my friend died.

"It was... no I can't describe it. I won't.

"When I recovered, he'd gone. He'd done his research though and we'd discussed what would happen if I failed, so I knew I had to get to him. Stop him. He'd become a monster. I won't bore you with the details but the only way to destroy him and save him was to burn his heart.

"I tracked him down to his office. The scene of the crime. He calmly let me in. Almost talked me into slitting my own throat. That silver tongue of his and a new lack of guilt, morals, remorse. A dangerous mix. The phone, I was literally saved by the bell. For whatever reason that broke his hold over me for long enough for me to sink my knife into his throat. No more beguiling words from him were going to be possible.

"His body emptied of animation. I will not call it life. Blood splashed the walls. And, yes, it was as lurid as PC Smith made out in his report. I started the proper ceremony little knowing that the phone call was from a neighbouring office that had seen me enter, stealthily, with my knife out, it was a warning call. They'd called the police too. When I saw the blue flashing lights I knew I'd have to work fast. Although you can't really rush a purification ritual. I had almost finished when they entered the room. Good job it wasn't an armed response unit I guess.

"So that's it. The truth. Yes, by the laws of the land, I killed him. I'm guilty. But it was the least I could do for failing him. I can see you don't believe me, still judging me. Well go on then.

"It's probably best that I'm locked up anyway. It might keep me safe. The purification ritual was disturbed. As I said, he's a monster now. He will come back."

ASH, BLOOD AND SNOW

THE CHILD WAS too excited by the snow to sleep. It had begun falling on the drive back from Nanny's. Fat, wet flakes that started to stick by the time they got home. There was no time for the child to play. The child's two siblings, older, not much wiser, could stay up for a couple of hours, but it was the child's bed time. The siblings went to play in the backyard.

The child's bedroom was at the front. Mother tucked the child in. The portable gas heater was plonked in the corner of the room, on high — whilst she read a story — turned down low when she left.

"You can play in the snow tomorrow," she said.

Tomorrow seemed like a long time away.

The child waited until the landing light was switched off and then stood on the bed, put its head behind the curtain and watched the snow.

Flakes swirled round the streetlight like ghostly moths around a candle flame. The child watched, entranced. The sound of the TV rose and fell like waves upon a shore. The bass rumble of the child's father as recognisable as the stale tobacco and sweat smell when the child was crushed against his chest.

The TV sound grew louder, then quieter, the door opening and closing. The siblings coming in, getting their goodnight drinks. When the landing light came on, the child dove back under the covers, pretending to sleep. Mother looked in briefly.

The light off again, the child imagined fun in the snow. The child had seen snow before, but it seemed like a very long time ago. It would make a snowman, and have snowball fights, and maybe, if Father could be persuaded, it would go sledding. The child's eyes slowly closed. Its breathing became more regular.

In the corner of the room the darkness swirled like a swarm of flies disturbed from a feast of shit. The child's piercing scream caused a bass rumble from downstairs, Father exclaiming something, naughty words probably. The TV noise became louder. Steps up the stairs, the third from the top creaking. The landing light on, the door opened, Mother and safety.

"Shhhh now. It's only a bad dream. Dreams can't hurt you. It's still snowing… look… you can wear all your warmest clothes tomorrow, and we'll go and play in the snow. But first you need to get some sleep. Shhh. The Darkman isn't coming. Isn't real, remember? We banished him together weeks ago didn't we? Shhh."

The child's cries subsided. Long enough for it to point to the corner of the room, but the swirling darkness had been banished by the light. Tucked in again, night light on, the door open a crack, the rumble of the Father's voice, a snatch of laughter and the TV noise. But again the child could not sleep.

The Darkman had been a recurring nightmare. A man? Swaddled and anonymous in ink black clothes, that came and stared at the child whilst it slept. Mother had banished it though. A candle against the darkness. A night light to keep it away.

The child watched the snow blanket the world in front of the house. Next door's black cab smudged out, blurred into a meaningless shape. The garden negated by white. The only colour in the street the orange penumbral glow of the streetlight and the flaking red painted wood of the identical council houses.

The world seemed to be holding its breath. The usual sounds of cats and dogs, birds, and people were muted.

There was a scrunching sound, like the marching of a miniature army, and a man walked into view, bundled up, long coat, woolly hat, scarf wrapped around his face, the same colour as the blizzard. First footprints on the virgin snow. The child watched the figure walk to the middle of the road where he stopped and turned to look at the child's house.

The man clapped, shook snow off himself, revealing clothes shockingly black against the whiteness of the snow. The Darkman! The child gasped and was too slow to duck to avoid the eyes of the Darkman which unerringly zeroed in on the window the child looked out of.

Overhead the birds that had made a nest in the house's eaves suddenly began flapping, agitated. The child's heart beat as fast as the time it had fallen in the water, before it knew how to swim. The child was transfixed. The Darkman shook like a dog, snow dusted the air around him. He slowly raised a hand, the fingers curling inward, until only one remained, a finger it placed where the mouth would be, if he even had a mouth. The child took a breath to scream again. The Darkman shook his head, turned and walked away. The child, swallowing its scream watched the black figure as far as it could. The Darkman walked into next door's garden, and the child heard the knock, knock, knock on the neighbour's door.

"Don't let him in. Don't invite him in. Don't… " The child murmured before the front door opened, there was a greeting, a low response and the door closed again. Next door had invited the Darkman in.

"Muuuuuuum!" the child cried, its scream now released. The roar of canned laughter preceded heavy footsteps up the stairs. The child's door opened fast.

"What's all this shouting about?" Father said coming into the room. "Hmmm?" A couple of short steps brought him to the child's bed, where he sat. The child lay down. "Your mother and

I are trying to watch TV. You need to go to sleep."

The child wanted to talk about the Darkman, but Father wouldn't understand. Only Mother knew. Instead the child nodded, let Father tuck it in, and snuggled down.

"Night night," Father said and closed the door behind him. The landing light off. The birds that lived in the eaves above the child's room — quiescent whilst Father had been there — started to make a fuss again. Voices rose next door.

There was a crash which jerked the child fully awake, jolted it into a sitting position. The child looked out, it couldn't see anything. The world was more white, the air a static of snow. The child panted like a wounded animal. The Darkman was making mischief next door!

The bedroom door opened, slowly, the child ducked beneath covers. "Make it go away," an uttered prayer.

"Are you awake?" a small voice whispered.

The child poked its head out. The siblings crept into the room. Eldest and Middle Child. Middle Child closed the door slowly, quietly.

"The Darkman is next door," the child said in a whisper to match Eldest.

"Don't be such a divvy. It's Kelly's nutter boyfriend," Eldest said. Kelly lived next door, an almost adult and occasional babysitter.

"Squidge up. We want to see," Eldest said as both siblings climbed onto the bed.

"I don't want to see," the child said.

"Then you'd best shut up and let us watch," Eldest said.

Middle Child virtually never said anything but left the child alone, mostly, unless Eldest was around. Middle Child always took Eldest's side. There was another crash next door. Raised voices. The sound of the front door opening.

"I think she's chucked him," Eldest announced.

The sound of scrunching again. The child decided it didn't want to see the Darkman again, didn't want the Darkman's gaze to sweep over it, didn't want to attract its attention.

"Hide… Please hide," the child said to the siblings.

Eldest snorted.

"He's stopped," Eldest said.

There was shouting outside. Bad words cut through the silence of the snow.

"Is the Darkman going?" the child asked.

"Shhhh," Middle Child hissed.

Eldest was engrossed.

There was a roar outside. Like nothing the child had ever heard before. There was rage in it, and loss, grief deeper than any the child had known, and pain, so much pain. The child wondered why the Darkman was so dark. The child shivered in fear.

There was the sound of glass smashing, and again, shockingly loud in the muffling air which was still swirling with snow. The child could see the sky, a uniform white, from where it lay. Hoping that the siblings would stop looking, they'd only attract the Darkman to them next.

Another loud shattering and an answering roar. This one just rage and incoherence.

"Uh-oh, Mick is coming out. Now he's for it," Eldest narrated. Mick was next door's Father. A black-cab driver, bullet head, thick neck, more tattoos than Father. Both siblings were breathing fast, the child gasped again. Eldest was red, Middle Child pale.

There was a shout, all the syllables smashed together, and the child risked a glance out of the window. Like two bull seals, Mick and the Darkman slammed against each other, chest to chest. Each snarling incoherent words. The Darkman was still covered by shadowy clothing. Mick was dressed in a garish red jumper. They were like blood and ash upon the snow.

"Make it stop. Make it go away. Make us safe," the child prayed.

"Shush you baby. I can't hear what they're saying," Eldest said still staring out the window. Middle Child just glared. It was a very good glare. Well practised. The child shut up. The child was quiet but terribly worried about Mick.

"He threw bricks through the windows!" Eldest's voice was filled with wonder. As though such an act of vandalism was the most perfectly wonderful thing they'd ever been witness to.

The shadows were suddenly painted bright blue.

"Moira must have called the police," Eldest announced. Moira was the mother next door.

The child's Mother and Father were obviously still downstairs, probably watching out of the front window. There was much more shouting. The child was just sneaking a peek when Mick threw the first punch. The Darkman didn't seem to move much but the punch flew well wide of the mark. The Darkman jerked, almost too fast for the eye to follow and Mick was on the ground. His jumper like a wound against the snow. Kelly screamed like it was her knocked to the ground. Eldest made an 'ooo' sound, and Middle Child sucked in a breath across a flash of teeth. The blue lights came closer.

"I'll be back!" the Darkman shouted. The whole of his lower face a blackness. The child thought the Darkman's eyes were upon the window where the children looked down upon the scene. "I'm coming for *you*," he shouted doing an about turn and sprinting away. The crunching of the snow marking his passage even when he was out of sight.

The police car arrived, and two policemen jumped out. The child heard the front door open, and Father was outside, muffled against the snow.

"Don't let Him in," the child said, still breathing hard.

Eldest knocked on the window and pointed down the road. The two policemen looked up, but so did Father. The police turned to look where Eldest was pointing, but Father narrowed his eyes and his face took on that 'you are in big trouble' look the three children knew so well.

The lights went out. Like someone had thrown a blanket over the street. Not a single house had lights, the TV's murmur stopped. The streetlights became dark. The blue flashing lights of the police car the only source of illumination, matched by the pale blue flame of the gas bottle heater.

"He's coming!" the child screamed.

'Shhhhh!' Eldest said.

Middle Child gulped.

The front door opened. There was a heavy tread on the stairs. Father stomped in.

"Right you three. To bed with you. We'll discuss your punishment tomorrow." He scooped up Middle Child and, hand on Eldest, steered the siblings out of the Youngest's room and into the one they shared. He leaned round the door briefly. "Bed!" he shouted. The child scooted into bed and pulled the covers up to its chin.

The door closed. Father clomped downstairs. Everything was still dark. The child closed its eyes and tried very hard to sleep. The blue flashing lights outside disappeared. The car reversing, and then driving away. But what about the Darkman?

The child stood once more and looked outside. The twilight world was painted white and thick flakes continued to fall. The child hugged itself and stood shivering, waiting for something to happen. Eventually, as the child's head grew heavy and rested against the deep cold of the window, its breath steaming the single glazed pane, the Darkman returned. Obviously not caught by the police.

The child jerked awake. The Darkman glanced up, spotted the child and repeated his finger against the mouth gesture from earlier. The black-clad figure walked calmly to the end of the road and disappeared down the alleyway between the houses. The Darkman was going to break in from the back.

The child needed a candle, it scooted over to its toy cupboard, opened a draw very slowly and found a stickle brick wand it had made a few days ago. The child knew that stickle bricks burned, it had tested this out previously on the gas canister heater, earning itself a severe telling off from Mother.

The stickle bricks burned with a greenish-blue flame and a

sweetly toxic smell. The child, after dripping hot melting plastic on its hand, held it at an angle. The drips falling on the carpet with tiny blue flashes of flame. The child walked softly to its parents' room, at the back of the house, the one overlooking the back yard, the makeshift candle a banishment for the Darkman.

When it got to Mother and Father's bedroom it pushed the pouffe over to the window and lifted up the net curtain. The child could not see the Darkman so held the improvised candle up high. Too high. With a whoosh the net curtain caught flame. The child stumbled backwards, falling from the pouffe, landing upon the floor with a bang, the improvised candle flying from its hand to land under the bed.

There was thumping up the stairs. "What the...?" Father's voice. The child spotted wisps of smoke coming from under the bed and crawled over to it, about to reach under, when thick black clouds started to roll out of the gap beneath it.

The child started crying. The door slammed open, and Father was there, he picked the child up and ran, across a smouldering carpet, the fastest the child had ever been carried, leaping downstairs. As soon as the child was on the floor Father shouted "Fire!" and ran back upstairs to rescue the other two children. Mother was suddenly in the hall. The front door thrown wide, the child's hand grabbed, the child dragged outside, into the freezing cold, the falling snow.

Father came out carrying Middle Child, Eldest in tow. The family turned to look back at the house. The fire was an insatiable monster rampaging through the upstairs. The child's bedroom ablaze, smoke gushing out of the top of the windows. The family took several steps backwards once the windows smashed from the heat and tongues of flame licked the roof. All the children were crying; Mother and Father seemed stunned. The child was warm on the front and freezing on the back. Stood in the deep snow with more settling in hair and nightclothes.

Neighbours from both sides ran out of their houses, a thin envelope between them and the hungry flames. Next door's windows gaped open, behind the one closest to the child's room was a baleful yellow glow. The fire having scuttled across the roof, setting Kelly's bedroom alight. When the Darkman appeared at the gaping hole, looking down on them, the child knew that Kelly had only just escaped. The child pointed to the Darkman who stood watching the people outside. The ends of the Darkman's black scarf whipped in the wind generated from the heat of the flames.

The child recognised that it had won. The Darkman was contained by the fire. That it would never haunt the child again. The child considered the loss of the house, its toys, its clothes, the TV, a small price to pay to be rid of the Darkman. Above the house two birds circled. Their empty nest lost to the flames. Ash spiralled into the sky to meet the vortex of snow being dumped by the clouds. Black and white swirled together. The child looked down as a flake of ash landed next to the splash of blood from where Mick had been punched.

"We should go in and get him," Father said to Mick who shook his head decisively. The Darkman pointed at the people outside. Towards the child, or so it thought, Kelly shouted "No!" and the Darkman turned, and walked into the flames.

Afterword

MOST OF THESE stories were written between 2013 and 2015, mostly for performance at various short story events in Bristol. I sent the book off with a great expectation that I could find a publisher and received an underwhelming response. That is until Piotr Swietlik suggested Kensington Gore. I knew that KG had published my friend Sarah Jayne Townsend so I found a home for the book. However KG wanted a novel from me too - since 'short stories from unknown authors don't sell.' I submitted a final MS of Magpies at the beginning of 2016 and KG published it very quickly. I then had only a couple of months to produce Sick City Syndrome for publication in October of the same year. Ironically Magpies has consistently outsold SCS ever since - whether through online sales or hand-selling at events. It was also shortlisted for the British Fantasy Award for Best Collection in 2017. So I obviously did something right here.

When KGHH (as Kensington Gore became) went out of business Grimbold Books (who also published my fantasy book Seven Deadly Swords) offered to do a reprint. This allowed me to look at it with fresh eyes. I've removed some stories that didn't fit the theme, added some that do so this is more a second edition than a reprint. I hope it continues to sell well and hope you've enjoyed it.

Pete W Sutton, Bristol 2020

Bonus Material

Seven Deadly Swords

Chapter 1

AVIGNON, FRANCE, 2012

REYMOND HUMMED ALOUETTE and sharpened his sword; this time the priest would die first. The rain hammered relentlessly upon the roof of the people carrier. He'd never got the hang of identifying machinery: it smelled new and it was red. He glanced out of the window into the night, seeing nothing, remembering deserts. His hands worked, a slow circular motion, comforting. He'd long since discovered that poetry and song soothed the constant rage. What was keeping Fisher?

Muscle memory took over and he contemplated the coming violence, the necessity of it. The priest had drawn him in, initially. It wasn't his fault, as such, but he held a fair measure of culpability. This time Reymond would end it. This time.

He was aware that he smiled grimly. How many times had he sworn that this time would be different, the last? He glanced back out the window. Avignon. So near where it had all started. Seat of popes. A fitting place to find the priest. The car was parked next to an ancient wall which stretched down the road to the priest's door. Where Fisher had gone some minutes ago. The priest would have had the dream, Reymond would be expected. Or one of them would be expected anyway. Dreams and portents, curses and sorcery. Reymond spat on the blade. This time he'd end it.

The sliding door of the car rattled open. Fisher, despite his bulk, and age, moved quietly: military training honed through many years of covert operations. Reymond raised an eyebrow at the Englishman who nodded and moved off, his yellow-white hair a flag in the dark. Reymond dropped the whetstone into its velvet bag, jumped out of the car and splashed through the wet clay mud covering the road to catch up with the larger man.

Once the big man was close enough for Reymond to see Fisher's cauliflower ears he asked, "And?"

"He's still there." The Merseyside accent seemed out of place here in France.

The priest's house was modest, a window onto Passage Saint Agricole, a door on Rue Felicient David. A courtyard interior. Sand-coloured stone. The priest's church, Saint Agricole, a short walk away.

The door swung open under Fisher's meaty hand and Reymond walked in ahead of the Englishman who held the door open for him. Reymond was struck again by the fact Fisher was approaching sixty. Soon to be too old for this work. Another good reason to end it this time.

The sound of prayer drifted down the stairs as the door swung shut behind Fisher. Reymond hefted his sword and followed the chant. The stairs were narrow and slippery, the plasterwork walls cracked and scabrous. A miasma of overcooked greasy food hung heavy on the air. Reymond continued to sing Alouette.

At the top of the stairs a nut-brown door stood open a crack. Latin spilled out. Reymond tightened his grip on the sword and pushed the door fully open. The short hallway he walked through, past a tiny kitchen, ended in a left turn into a sitting room. Waist-high bookcases flanked the door and ahead was a well-used sofa of cracked brown leather. The Latin abruptly stopped.

"Reymond. And Mr Fisher. Welcome."

"It's just Fisher."

The priest sat at a dining table, a bottle of single malt in front of him, empty glasses waiting. "I wasn't sure if Fisher would be joining us." He picked up the bottle and screwed the top off, pouring a generous measure into each glass.

Reymond's gaze roved the room: he narrowed his eyes and tried to ignore the siren song of fury that bubbled just beneath the surface. "After everything. After..." Reymond's hand, the one not holding the sword, made an abortive gesture. "You still believe?"

The priest followed Reymond's eyes to where his own hand had picked up a set of mahogany beads and a silver crucifix. A simple enough rosary, well-made, expensive, but not ostentatious.

"It is ever a mystery to me that you no longer do, Reymond. You were always a great believer." The priest picked up his glass, his finger and thumb counting beads. The glass shook as he raised it to his lips.

Fisher crossed the room and took the offered glass. With a glance at Reymond he knocked back the whisky, then sat to one side and kicked the chair opposite the priest out as an invitation to Reymond.

"You don't think that all we've seen proves that He has no plan for us?" Reymond asked.

The priest shrugged. "We are what God has made us."

Reymond barked a humourless laugh. "And what is that exactly? Father."

"If your dreams and times in between are as mine then I think you know."

"You know nothing." Reymond took a step towards the table. He could feel his control slipping: he bit his lip and started reciting Dante under his breath.

The priest held out the rosary. "Come, Reymond. Pray with me, like we used to. It will give you comfort, like at Dorylaeum."

Reymond's sword flicked out, and the beads rattled across the table and onto the flagstone floor. "It is time," he snarled.

Pete W. Sutton

Interviewed by

Jessica Rydill

JR - Your first book, *A Tiding of Magpies*, was shortlisted in 2017 for Best Collection at the British Fantasy Awards. The collection takes its name from a children's rhyme which itself has an ominous flavour. What is the significance of the magpies – and the stories?

PWS - It all started with the first story in the collection – Roadkill – which is about a creepy boy who counts roadkill during a car journey. I used the counting rhyme as a structure for that story. I then wrote a story called Thunder and Magpies where I returned to the theme of the counting rhyme with a creepy family. The last piece that slotted in was a Visual Verse story called Waymarker. For Visual Verse you are given a picture prompt and have to write a story based on the picture. Waymarker was based on a picture of a pile of dead birds which looked like a waymarker, you know, the piles of balanced stones people leave in certain places. I wrote a serial killer flash and based on the picture I needed a name for the killer to fit the picture and so the

Seventh Magpie was born. I recognised I was obviously writing to a theme and started to think which of my stories would fit a collection based on that theme - I wrote some specifically for the book and then looked for a publisher…

JR - Your most recent novel, *Seven Deadly Swords*, was published in October 2018 by Grimbold Books, which publishes us both. The book tells the story of an accursed crusader seeking to free himself from the curse through time. What was the inspiration for the story and what drew you to the historical era of the Crusades?

PWS - I read The Crusades Through Arab Eyes by Amin Maalouf in the 90's and a lot of what was in that book was interesting – our history seen from a very different perspective. There is a particular piece of history though – the battle for Ma'Arra – that I'd not come across before which became the pivotal part of the plot. Reymond and his brothers in arms came from a Vampire The Masquerade campaign I ran in the 90's which used the seven deadly sins and the battle of Ma' Arra. In 2013 when I first started writing the book the Syrian civil war was at its height and certain people in the West were talking about another crusade.

JR - The protagonist, Reymond, is doomed to immortality as a personification of one of the Seven Deadly Sins. What can you tell us about Reymond and his quest for redemption?

PWS - Reymond is a farmer at the beginning of the book. He is radicalised by a priest so that he becomes a zealot who joins up to fight the great foe of the time –the Muslims. War isn't this great quest for glory he thinks it is and as the campaign grinds on and the battles take more and more of the crusader force he grows slowly disillusioned. But because of the choices he made when he was a zealot he is cursed, along with six others. The book mainly tells how he tries to break the curse.

JR - You have edited two anthologies for Grimbold Books: Science Fiction anthology *Infinite Dysmorphia*, which you edited with Kate Coe, in May 2018, and Fantasy anthology *Forgotten Sidekicks*, which you edited with Steven Poore, in April 2020. What are the special demands and pleasures of editing an anthology?

PWS - I like that each anthology is different – I've edited eight so far. Choosing the stories is a demand, and a pleasure. Making sure the book works, like a good music album, with stories placed well is also both demanding and rewarding. And working with other editors is a great experience. Being able to bring out a story and make it the best it can be in collaboration with an author is the main draw for me.

JR - Your short fiction has appeared in many magazines and anthologies, from *Airship Shape and Bristol Fashion* from Wizard's Tower Press to *The Alchemy Press Book of Horrors 2*, and many more. What is the distinction between writing short stories and novels, and what creative possibilities does each form offer?

PWS - I think the aim of a short story is to deliver a unity of purpose in a single sitting whereas a novel can explore something over a much longer period. But it's not just about length – there is a level of complexity that can be supported at novel-length that's just not possible with a short. Some people are better at long form, others at short form and a rare few can do both with equal accomplishment. I tend to brevity, I'm an underwriter and I feel more comfortable in short form – you can do things in a short, experimentally, you'd never be able to sustain in a novel. Especially at flash length (which is where I started off really). It's much harder to make a mark as a purely short story writer though (unless you're Borges!)

JR - You are a contributing editor at *Far Horizons* magazine, can you tell us more about that?

PWS - Far Horizons started on Facebook as a few people in a writing social group decided to write an anthology together.

The idea quickly morphed into doing a monthly magazine and although there were plenty of keen writers there wasn't anyone with editing experience. I'd done an MA in Publishing at Oxford Brookes back in the day, which included modules in proofreading and copyediting so I dug my notes out and volunteered to edit the magazine. I think you can probably tell that the first few issues are quite rough but like writing the more you edit the better you get at it. The lady who started it off was Australian and had this idea that the magazine would never reject a story – which was very, very tough, because some writers need an awful lot of coaching to become publication worthy. However this both developed me as an editor and as a writer. So although some stories in those mags would never sell to a professional market I'm still glad I did it. The writers came from all over as did the volunteer staff (Australia, UK, USA, Russia and Macedonia) which presented challenges with timezones and deadlines. Eventually we did three anthologies which also taught me a lot about publishing and then the staff got pulled in different directions and issues started getting delayed, so we cut the number of issues and we still found it hard to hit deadlines so eventually it went on hiatus –and as yet hasn't come out of it. I'm still firm friends with lots of folks I met through that magazine and I'm editing a novel from one of the writers and waiting on another to finish their book so Far Horizons Press will probably return to bring a couple of books out.

JR - What is the importance of Grimdark Fantasy and why is it so popular and relevant today? What does the name "Grimdark" mean to you?

PWS - Some people said that Seven Deadly Swords was Grimdark. I guess because bad things happen to most of the characters it could be. I've not read much epic fantasy over the last twenty years or so (I did read a lot of it as a teenager though) and I guess Grimdark was a breath of fresh air after Noble Bight (retroactively named I assume) but to my mind if the palette is all black it's just as dull as if the palette is all white. I'm thinking that since the world has moved on somewhat people will be hankering after some 'nicer' stories and that Grimdark is going to wane, just like dystopias are going to. Maybe.

JR - You recently delivered your latest book, *A Certainty of Dust*, to Grimbold. Can you tell us about the novel and what your readers can expect?

PWS - The Certainty of Dust is Jacob's Ladder directed by Death from The Seventh Seal; a dark thriller about a young woman trying to save her sister's soul from oblivion with only the power of song. Jackie and Beth, sisters and bandmates in The Orpheus Head, are involved in a motorbike accident driving home from a gig. Death visits them as they lie, broken and bleeding, on the asphalt and offers Jackie a challenge in order to save her sister from annihilation. She must make the undertaker Massicott cry using just her music and needs to gain her sister's forgiveness, for a wrong she has done her - before it's too late. Jackie is given a little over a month, until St Lucy's day, to complete the trial.

It's set in the modern day and is a bit of a psychological study really. There are some creepy parts too though.

JR - You are an active organiser of the Bristol Festival of Literature and of BristolCon Fringe. Can you tell us about that, reflecting on last year and the future?

PWS - I'm afraid I'm not now, nor ever have been, an organiser of BristolCon Fringe (which seems to have stopped now anyway) – I was on the committee for BristolCon in the past but wasn't last year – so not much to say about that except to say that BristolCon is a great one day con, very friendly, well-organised and a must on the circuit.

I've been a co-organiser of Bristol Festival of Literature (BFL) since 2012. I do try to ensure that Bristol Festival of Literature doesn't treat genre as badly as some other lit fests and we had a very successful year last year. This year we'll be returning with a digital festival I think – given the pandemic. We try to be very grassroots and supportive of local talent both well-known names and unknown names. We see our job being to equip, engage and inspire the city with literature.

JR - With your latest book delivered to the publisher, what are you working on now?

PWS - Grimbold have kindly offered to republish A Tiding of Magpies so I'm making sure that that's up to date and there'll probably be a couple of new stories in the reprint. I'm also working to complete my next short story collection (tentatively titled The Museum for Forgetting) and I'm going to try and get a few short stories published. I'm just starting research on the next book which I'll probably be ready to start writing early next year – it'll be another historical one so lots of reading about the time period.

JR - What are you reading and what have you been enjoying over the past year?

PWS - I read over a hundred books a year most years (and I still have a massive TBR). I'm quite an eclectic reader too. Books I've really enjoyed this year include Horse Destroys the Universe by Cyriak Harris, The Liar's Dictionary by Eley Williams, Eden by Tim Lebbon, Consider This by Chuck Palahnuik (a writing advice book), The Price you Pay by Aidan Truhan and The Book of Koli by Mike Carey

JR - Are politics important to your writing and can writing ever be apolitical?

PWS - Anyone who follows me on Twitter will know that I get too involved with politics. I don't think it's possible to be apolitical in life, or in letters – any attempt to be so is a political act and all stances towards any sort of moral position is a political statement. I need to get better at channeling my anger at our political situation into writing.

JR - When not reading or writing, what are you watching on TV, or bingeing on Netflix or Prime?

PWS - I don't watch a lot of television, I tend to watch a film or two a week. TV wise I really enjoyed Tales from the Loop and have just started watching Castle Rock. I've also been watching Doom Patrol and rewatching Supernatural from the beginning.

JR - How has the lockdown affected your writing, and has it brought benefits as well as problems for you as a writer?

PWS - Not sure it has – ask me again in a month's time. I've been so concentrating on getting the novel finished that I didn't really stop to contemplate being locked down. But then I've been working throughout the lockdown and not much has changed about that for me.

JR - You are stranded on a desert island. What seven books do you take?

PWS - Just seven? Hmm As I said earlier I read over 100 books a year most years. Are you sure I can't bring a Kindle pre-loaded with 100's of books and some way to generate electricity? So I'd want chunksters. The Weird Compendium by Jeff and Ann VanderMeer, the complete Jorge Luis Borges, The Procrastinator's diary (because I haven't got round to using it yet), a thick notebook to write my own stories so I don't run out of reading material – even if it's my own work, Guards, Guards by Terry Pratchett (which isn't a chunkster but is very re-readable), Possibly one of the Russians – Dostoyevsky probably and Under the Dome by Stephen King –that's his longest, right?

Copyright

'Roadkill' first published in *The Speculative Book* 2016
'The Stone Of Sorrow' © Pete W Sutton 2020
'The Night Market' © Pete W Sutton 2020
'Married in Blue' © Pete W Sutton 2020
'Le Sacre du Printemps' © Pete W Sutton 2020
'Across The Border' © Pete W Sutton 2020
'Bruised' first published in Far Horizons 2014
'The Infection' first published in Far Horizons 2014
'It's always the end for someone' first published in *Apocalypse Chronicles* from Almond Press 2016
'The Soft Spiral of a Collapsing Orbit' first published in Far Horizons 2015
'It Falls', Winner of the SciArt weird ecology writing competition & first published in SciArt, June 2014
'Five For Silver' © Pete W Sutton 2020
'The Case of the Murders in the Rue Morgue' © Pete W Sutton 2020
'The Amnesia-Ridden Hills' © Pete W Sutton 2020
'Waymarker' first published in Visual Verse 2014

'The Cat's Got It' first published on Storieswithpictures.com 2014
'Not Alone' © Pete W Sutton 2020
'I Butler' © Pete W Sutton 2020
'Six Geese A-Laying' first published in *Twelve Days of Christmas* from KGHH 2017
'You Have Reached Your Destination' first published on the British Fantasy Society Monthly Story 2018
'Have you heard the magpies singing?' first published on National Flash Fiction Day's Flash Flood 2013
'White Noise, Black Silence' first published on 1000 words 2013
Thunder and Magpies © Pete W Sutton 2020
'Spin, Spin, Spin, the Wheel of Justice' © Pete W Sutton 2020
'Ash, Blood and Snow' first published in Far Horizons 2016
'Seven Deadly Swords' published by Grimbold Books 2018